Dead-Eye and Job entered the opening and made their way down the stone steps that led to the catacombs beneath the ceremonial kiva. The gunfighter's foxfire eye cast a yellow glow upon the surrounding walls and the descending stairs, illuminating the way. A moment later, they stepped through a lower doorway and found themselves facing an unnerving tableau.

Missy Slatter was hogtied and laying atop the stone altar, writhing and thrashing. At the head of the sacrificial slab stood Vasco Núñez. The dark priest was decked out in ebony robes, his hands raised over head as he chanted an incantation in an unknown tongue. His face was rigid and gleamed with sweat, while his eyes were bright with an unholy fervor. One of his outstretched hands was empty, while the other held an ornate dagger with a wickedly long blade.

"Look!" said Job. "Along the walls!" The mummified remains of Gaspar Espejo and his conquistadors hung motionlessly at first. Then, slowly, they began to jerk, their joints creaking and the bones trapped within the confinement of leather wrapping rattling with protest, aching to be free. Their neckbones popped and crackled as their heads rotated, regarding the young victim atop the altar with empty eye sockets.

At the same time, Dead-Eye saw that the child had slowly ceased her fighting. She grew limp upon the altar. Her robust face turned as pale as lard and her blue eyes, customarily full of piss and vinegar, became glassy and unfocused. "What's he doing to Lil' Miss?" he asked in alarm.

"The bastard's siphoning away her life force!" Job told him. "Transferring it to those carcasses on the walls!" As they started forward, the negro noticed that Núñez had ceased his chanting. Both hands entwined tightly around the haft of the dagger now. "He's intent on completing the ritual with a blood sacrifice!"

The Saga of

DEAD-EYE

BOOK THREE

Man-Eaters, Mummies, & Murderous Maniacs

by RONALD KELLY

Book Three: *Man-Eaters, Mummies,*
& Murderous Maniacs
is dedicated to the following folks:

Brennan LaFaro
James Lawson Moore
Vivian Kasley
Zach McCain
&
Justin T. Coons

Chapter One

The Chihuahua Desert, Mexico
Late December 1869

Time is like a knife. If used wisely, if kept oiled and the edge honed sharply, it is a tool that does its job constructively, skillfully, without a moment's regret. Endless, playful summer days as a child, blissful evenings of courting on a porch swing in the moonlight, the restful afternoons of the aged, dozing and softly awaiting the comforting whisper of Old Man Death in their ear.

If used foolishly, time becomes a burden. Rust-laden and dulled to uselessness. Sometimes slowed to a creep by guilt or anger or the desire for retribution. It is then that the single ticking of a clock seems like the length of a day or more. An eternity. Walking in place until your feet grow raw with sores and not a mile of purpose gained.

It had become like that for Dead-Eye and Job. The broad, sunbaked expanse of the Chihuahua was a constant and unchanging thing, from sunrise to sundown. Mile upon mile, a fiery orb glared down at them from above, unblinking, blistering their flesh, even beneath the shelter of cloth and hat felt. The animals they rode—the black roan Brimstone and the white mule Balaam—trudged onward as well, knowing who they sought and understanding the urgency of finding them.

They soon became legend in the barren territory. The small black man, bald as a billiard ball with a picket of gold and silver teeth, dressed in a dusty derby hat, a vest with pockets aplenty, and necklaces laden with voodoo talisman and charms.

And, with him, the tall man in black from the South, toting a sawed-down twelve-gauge and a nickel-plated Colt Dragoon. Grim and emaciated, looking and smelling like the ripest of death, with a thick dark mustache and eyes that were mismatched twins; one cold and steel gray, the other blind and glowing eerily beneath the brim of his hat with the luminance of foxfire.

Every now and then, the two riders would happen across someone on the trail. A man traveling alone, a pair of soldiers journeying home, or a family in a buckboard, and they would ask the question. "Have you heard tell of an outlaw named Jules Holland, traveling with three rough hombres, and a woman in a wagon, both as black as coal?" And, more often than not, they would reply "Yes," and tell them of their sinister exploits, and that they had been seen a few towns ahead, not very long ago.

And, so, the lanky gunfighter with flesh as pale as lard and the negro mojo man would continue onward, believing that the distance between them and their prey had shortened considerably and that what they had set out to do would finally be accomplished within the span of a day's ride.

But it never came to pass. That day's ride turned into three, then stretched into weeks and months. And they seemed no closer than they had been at the very beginning of their journey.

It was on a cold night, while camping in a dry wash surrounded by a thorny stand of mesquite and thistle, that she came to him in a dream.

"Papa."

Job opened his eyes and saw her standing there, no more than six feet away from where he lay. Tall and lean, but generous in the hips and bodice, much like her late mother. Clad head to toe in black taffeta and lace, her face scarcely visible beneath a dark veil. Holding that confounded book in her black-gloved hands, the unholy tome that called forth demons, ogres, and dragons, and left sickness, misery, and death in the wake of her footsteps.

"Evangeline," he said, at first startled to see her. But soon, his surprise and

confusion subsided. "Dream-walking now, are you?"

She stared at him and smiled slyly. It was a gesture much like a carrion crow appraising a dying dog on a roadway. "You must turn back, dear father," she cautioned. "Abandon this nonsense and return to the swamp to live out your days in peace and solitude." She looked over at where the tall Southerner with the sunken face and the glowing eye sat against a boulder across the campfire, oblivious to her presence. "Lift that foolish voodoo spell of yours and allow that poor soul to roam the Earth no longer. Let him fly with the angels, or burn with the damned, whichever his fate might be."

Job sat up from his blankets and regarded her sternly. "No, daughter. As long as Holland and his men plague good and decent men, as long as you crack open realms and unleash Hell upon this world... we will be dogging your heels. And, sooner or later, we will catch up and bring this trail of travesty and perversion to an end."

Evangeline laughed. "Oh, Papa! You've had ample time and opportunity to do that, but still you ride, mile after countless mile, and your prize always eludes you. Why is that? Why do we always seem to be so far away?" Pity almost shown in the dark eyes behind the sheer. "Perhaps your cause is hopeless and futile. Perhaps you and the black-hearted corpse you ride with are not yet worthy to reach the promised land."

"We'll get there eventually," the little black man declared. "And then the evil you and the others have cursed mankind with will be dead and done. And you, my child, with it."

The ebony woman shook her head in curt dismissal. Her hands caressed the leather of the book called Necronomicon, causing the flesh of it to ripple and prickle with gooseflesh. "This is my final warning, Papa. Turn around and ride home. Find serenity in the bayou that gave you birth. Grow old and die with contentment... not with terror and dread, on a nameless trail, with the minions of my conjuring at your throat."

Job was about to speak again, but abruptly she was gone. The willowy apparition of his youngest daughter had retreated to wherever she presently rested her head and ended her stroll within his slumber.

The following morning, before another day's riding, Job crouched before the fire and poured himself a cup of coffee, as black and bitter as he was.

"How long have we been in this desert?" he asked his traveling companion. "A month? Six months? A year or more?"

Dead-Eye stared at him and considered the question for a moment. "I can't rightly say. The passage of time is lost to the dead, you know."

"And it's been lost to me as well," the negro answered solemnly. He looked over at Dead-Eye's roan, standing next to Job's white mule. The eyes of the demon-possessed horse glowed a muted crimson, but not as brightly as they once had. "Another thing… do you recall how Ol' Brimstone could track the animals of Holland and the others from the very beginning? Could smell its own kind and sense exactly which direction they were heading? But now he's bumfuzzled and unable to do so?"

"Yes. I've been pondering that myself," said the zombie. Curiously, he eyed the man across the fire. "What's happened that's gotten you so dadblamed introspective this morning?"

Job hesitated, then continued. "She came to me in a dream last night. Evangeline. Warned me to abandon our quest. Told me to turn tail and run home to the bayou. Said that if we didn't, misfortune of the worst sort would befall us."

"But it was only a dream, wasn't it?"

"No. She was here, alright. I thought her incapable of dream-walking, but she did it, by God. Invaded my sleep and left her ultimatum." His dark brow furrowed as a thought came to mind. "And, I'm believing, a clue to our predicament as well."

Dead-Eye couldn't figure out what the little man was referring to. "What sort of predicament?"

"Roaming this godforsaken desert for as long as we can recollect, that's what." He reached into a pocket of his vest and brought out his book of spells and incantations. Intently, he flipped through the yellowed pages. "I'm thinking I know precisely what sort of black magic she's spun upon us."

"And what would that be?"

Job stopped at a page and nodded to himself. "Just as I suspected. We've been victims of an Exodus Curse."

Dead-Eye was more perplexed than ever. "What in tarnation is that?"

"Do you recall in the Bible how Moses delivered the Israelites from Egypt, but due to their bull-headed insolence and lack of faith, the Lord condemned them to walk in the desert for forty years, before they reached the Land of Milk and Honey?"

"Yes. I do remember that tale."

"Well, scholars of the Good Book claim that the distance between Egypt and the Promised Land, or Canaan, was no more than two hundred miles. That meant they should have walked that stretch on foot in eleven days' time. But, instead, it took forty years of hardship and steady traveling."

"You're saying they walked around in a circle for four decades before the Lord bestowed their reward? All on account of their bitching and moaning and raising up golden calves and such?"

Job's picket of silver and gold teeth caught morning sunlight as he grinned. "I am. And, believe it or not, that's precisely what we've been doing for God knows how long. She cast that spell upon us and we've been wandering through the Mexican desert with no true sense of time or direction. I'd bet my bottom dollar that those we came across in our travels were put there to mislead us, too. No more than mirage images telling us we were fast on the trail, when we were probably hundreds of miles away from those we pursued."

"Shitfire!" cursed Dead-Eye. "And you're saying she could actually do such a thing?"

"Not only could she, but she did." He studied the page of the book closely, his brown eyes twinkling. "But I think I can undo it. I believe I can lift this curse and we'll be back to our senses and back on track once again."

"Well, what are you waiting for? Commence to hoodooing!"

Quickly, they gathered their bedrolls and supplies, then mounted their rides and left the stand of desert bramble. They stood upon the flat, merciless expanse of the Chihuahua and regarded their surroundings. All four directions—north, south, east, and west—looked identical, with only meager changes in the landscape.

"Gonna try something here," said Job. The little man tugged the reins of Balaam, causing the albino mule to slowly turn in a complete circle. Oddly enough, everywhere he looked was sunrise. "No wonder we weren't getting anywhere. The position of the sun and stars was an illusion all along."

"Some powerful magic she conjured," said Dead-Eye in amazement.

"Indeed." Job propped the little book open against the horn of his saddle and dug through several pockets of his vest until he found a compass. He eyed its needle and determined that the direction they faced was due south. Whether that was the true direction or not couldn't be rightfully determined. "Hold firm to Brimstone and try not to move. This is liable to get a mite tumultuous."

The mojo man lifted the compass over his head and began to chant an incantation from the book. As the needle of the compass began to spin, slowly, then building in speed, the dust of the earth around them did the same. It rose and began to blow in a counterclockwise manner, growing in intensity. Soon, they found themselves in the heart of a massive dust devil. As the maelstrom reached the pinnacle of its fury, the grit of sand and rock pelted them like buckshot and the currents of the wind nearly wrenched them bodily from their saddles. Then, as the spoken incantation came to a close, the bluster ceased and the earth settled around them.

"Well?" asked Dead-Eye, brushing dust and debris from the shoulders of his frock coat. "Did it work?"

A low, thunderous snort from the black horse answered his question. Brimstone's eyes blazed a brilliant crimson, and dark smoke and cinder expelled forcefully from his flaring nostrils. Abruptly, he whirled on his hooves and faced the opposite direction from which they had been headed.

Job studied the position of the compass's needle and grinned. "Looks like we're heading north."

Without hesitation, they started in that direction at a steady canter.

"Job?"

The negro regarded the man riding beside him. Dead-Eye's mustachioed face was sullen and uneasy, even more brooding than usual. "You're concerned about the boy, aren't you?"

Dead-Eye considered Daniel, who had been abducted by the vampire Holland shortly after the War Between the States—his only son, who he had been in search of even before his untimely death in a lonesome clearing back in Tennessee. "What has this confounded deception of time cost us?" he asked. "Have they killed him, or has Holland turned him into one of his own?" A distant memory flashed before his eyes—his lovely wife, Elizabeth, confronting him in the cellar of a Georgia mansion, fangs bared and eyes full of bloodlust. One of Holland's countless victims, abandoned and left to fend for herself in the most ghastly of ways.

"All we can do is hope and pray that it hasn't yet come to that," Job told him. "But, if we find the boy and it has come to pass, you know what you must do."

Dead-Eye said nothing in reply. The iron of determination replaced the sadness in his gaze and he laid his heels to Brimstone's hindquarters, quickening his pace.

The little man from Louisiana nodded and did the same, catching up in a trot. *So be it, then*, he thought. *Let's leave this hell and ride for the promised land.*

Chapter Two

**Piedras Negras, on the border of Mexico and Texas
February 1870**

Puzzled, Job leaned forward in his saddle and squinted at a small village on the horizon. "Is that fog up ahead?" he asked. It was a frigid afternoon and the mojo man wore his coat of many skins—made of fox, possum, squirrel, raccoon, and cat, among others—as well as a pair of moleskin muffs to warm his ears.

Dead-Eye, who had no body temperature to surrender, sat astride Brimstone in the broadcloth suit he'd worn for the past four years. "At this time of day?" His good eye narrowed as he surveyed the settlement they approached. To either side of the gathering of buildings it was clear, but amid the structures there seemed to hang a thick mist. "I've seen this sort of thing before... or so I'll know for sure once we get there." He laid his hand across the butt of his .44 pistol. "Keep iron close at hand. We could be facing something mighty hellacious."

As they moved forward, Job shucked his Henry rifle from its scabbard and levered a round into the breech. In turn, Dead-Eye disengaged the sling of the sawed-down shotgun from beneath his coat and hung it on the horn of Brimstone's saddle. He was already aware that the horse beneath him had sensed that something was amiss up ahead. Dead-Eye could feel the muscle and bone beneath the demon-animal's ebony hide begin to take on heat, like a furnace stoked and set ablaze.

Soon, they had reached the edge of town. Job studied what lay ahead, his dark hands clutching the repeating rifle tightly. He felt a shudder of dread run through him from the nape of his neck to the tip of his tailbone.

"I do declare!" he muttered softly. "It isn't mist a'tall. It looks like…"

Dead-Eye drew his revolver from its holster. "Cobwebs."

They halted several yards from the first cluster of buildings and regarded the little village named Piedras Negras. Along the rutted street stood a dozen wooden structures—a mercantile, a hotel, and a cantina, among others. Further on were a scattering of homes and at the very end of the avenue was a church. A large adobe mission house with stained-glass windows and a bell tower with a cross of hammered bronze upon its crown.

Stretching between the buildings were vast strands of a pale, silky substance, from one roof to another, clinging thickly from porch awnings and railings, choking doorways and windows. Dead-Eye took a silver dollar from his coat pocket and flipped it between thumb and forefinger. The coin spun through the air, caught in the sticky substance, and clung there.

As they rode onward, ducking so their hats would not be ensnarled, they found several large pods of the satiny material lying on the ground in front of the livery stable. Passing by, Brimstone gritted his teeth and snorted.

"What do you reckon those are?" wondered Job.

"Horses," Dead-Eye told him flatly. "Do you recall me telling you of what I discovered in a stand of pines near Chattanooga, back before you resurrected me and turned me into a walking dead man?"

"The sheriff and his posse?" A chill ran through the mojo man that had nothing to do with the winter weather. "You mean to tell me…?"

The gunfighter nodded. "Yes. The creature from the Hole Out of Nowhere. Conjured by your darling daughter." He remembered how he had found the leader of the posse, Elmer Bradley, suspended in a vast web in the pine grove—eyeless, nearly sucked dry of his fluids, a breath or so from his very last. *Mymahthu!* he had rasped as his vocal cords crumbled like rotten twine. *That was the name it proclaimed…prideful and vindictively… like a god before maggots.*

"Where do you suppose everyone is?" asked Job. The street was deserted and the businesses standing on either side seemed empty and abandoned.

"I have no idea," said Dead-Eye. He didn't have to spur Brimstone forward. The black horse started down the street of his own accord, as though drawn by some unknown influence. "Let's take a look-see, but keep your eyes sharp." His grip tightened on the .44 Dragoon, thumb resting lightly on the hammer, ready to cock.

The snow-white mule quickened his pace until he was beside Brimstone, matching him step for step. Dead-Eye and Job sat tall in their saddles, alert, their nerves wound as tightly as a pocket watch spring. Around and above them, broad sheets of silky webbing stretched from pillar to post. Several times they spotted small, shriveled forms dangling within the sticky substance. Dogs, cats, a buzzard or two who had sensed the lingering stench of death and flown too closely. They surveyed the buildings as they passed, but only darkness and silence dwelt within their hollows. Nary a living thing could be detected.

Brimstone tossed his head and snorted, sending a spray of hot ash and cinder into the gray winter air. Dead-Eye looked ahead and saw that the double doors of the adobe structure at the end of the street were standing wide open. "The church," he said. Allowing the horse to move onward without prompting, the gunfighter looped the reins around the saddle's horn, then took the sawed-down scattergun and cracked open the double breach. He checked the loads. Both shells were packed with gunpowder and slugs of solid silver.

He closed the shotgun with a snap and found that they had stopped no more than twenty feet from the mission's entrance. "You ready to go in?"

Job nodded solemnly and, together, they swung to the ground and headed for the open doorway. Dead-Eye toted the big hogleg pistol in one pale, blue-veined hand and the stubby twelve-gauge in the other, while Job clutched the Henry repeater, two-fisted, aiming from the hip.

A few feet from their destination, Dead-Eye's boot struck something, causing it to roll unevenly across the earth. He looked down to discover that it was the fleshless skull of a small child.

The dead man looked over at the swamp sorcerer. Job's features were grim and unflinching, but Dead-Eye knew him well enough to sense that he was spooked. And, to tell the honest truth, so was he.

As one, they stepped through the doorway... and cast their eyes upon what awaited them.

"Good God Almighty!" Job gasped, dumbfounded.

Dead-Eye lifted his single good eye from the rows of wooden pews to the rafters high above them. He said nothing in exclamation, for what they encountered was precisely what he had expected to find.

Entangled in a massive cobweb above their heads were the citizens of Piedras Negras. Men, women, and children, perhaps fifty or more in number... strung up, their limbs contorted in fright and agony. Their empty eye sockets stared blindly down at them, faces sunken and dry as dust, mouths screaming silently in a rictus of absolute terror.

"I've heard tell of the demon god named Mymathu all my life," the practitioner of voodoo and black magic muttered. "But until this very moment, I never realized how wicked and depraved it really was."

Dead-Eye lowered his eyes from the cathedral of corpses and stared at something behind the pulpit at the rear of the sanctuary. "What is that yonder?"

Job followed his gaze and was startled to see that the rear wall of the holy place had been desecrated. Hanging on the wall had been a large wooden cross bearing a sculpture of the crucified Christ. Something had bitten off the head of Jesus, chewed it up, and spat it away in contempt. It had also left something scrawled across the adobe wall in broad, slashing streaks of human blood.

"I've never seen anything like it before," Dead-Eye said, attempting to decipher the symbols of unknown tongue and origin.

"I have." Job took the little leatherbound book from his pocket and flipped to a page at the very back. Taking the stub of a lead pencil from a vest pocket, he began to compare the otherworldly etchings with what showed on a yellowed page of the journal, then jotted the translation down in the margin. When he was finished, he showed the message to the man standing beside him.

TO THOSE IN PURSUIT, BE FOREWARNED!
FLEE OR BE TORMENTED AND FEASTED UPON!
THUS DECLARES MYMATHU!

Dead-Eye considered the notice and grunted. "They sure do leave us some godawful warnings, don't they?" He recalled one left for them near the banks of the Mississippi River, an unfortunate farmer nailed to an oak tree with railroad spikes, the words HEAVEN, HELL, and CATASTROPHE carved into his flesh.

"They surely do," admitted Job, ruminating on the same hideous memory. "And innocent folks keep dying because of it. Because of *us*."

"They keep dying in spite of us as well," the Southerner told him. "If we were dead and buried, or turned tail and skedaddled, they'd still continue with their torturing and killing. Like it or not, we're the only ones who can find them and put an end to it."

The negro's eyes were doubtful. "Are we? Do we really have a chance to stop this kind of evil and atrocity? Dark gods who are summoned from other realms to slaughter entire towns without a shred of conscience, just to dissuade us from our mission?"

"You've faced such demons before and defeated them," Dead-Eye reminded him. "Back in Bogalusa Parish. When you put an end to Rosemonde and Evangeline's reign of terror."

"You're right," allowed Job, "but..."

The gunfighter leveled a skeletal finger at the mojo man. "Don't lose your piss and vinegar now, you runty, little rooster!" he said, choosing his words carefully. "You're the one who set this journey into motion… the one who resurrected my gunshot and mutilated carcass and turned it into a dealer of vengeance and death. If you take leave of your nerve now, what will become of your daughter? Who will put an end to the wickedness and iniquity she conjures with a word on her lips or a wave of her hand? And what about my son? What about young Daniel? Is he to die at the hands of those fiends, or be turned into one himself, from the bite of the man who stole him?"

Job nodded as he chewed on the harsh words that had been fed to him. "Yessir, you're correct." He straightened his spine, adding an inch or two to his stature. "We have no time to lose our resolve or have misgivings about our task. Let's leave this place and get back to the trail."

Dead-Eye stared up at the bodies that hung above their heads. "Don't seem proper, abandoning them in such a sorry state."

"I know… it feels like a blasphemy," agreed Job. "But we have no way of physically reaching them and the winter earth is too frozen for burying." He stood there silently for a moment, then walked to the front of the church, where a bank of votives stood behind the pulpit and below the ghoulish warning. He found a brass receptacle with long-handled matches, struck one, and lit a single candle. As he turned around, an expression of great sorrow creased his dark face. "I'd say most of these poor souls are already walking the golden streets of Paradise. A holy place like this seems like a fitting tomb for their earthly remains… at least for the time being."

Together, the two left the adobe building and respectfully closed the heavy, oaken doors behind them.

Dead-Eye considered the abomination called Mymathu. "You know we'll encounter that spider-legged son of a bitch, face to face, before it's over and done with."

Job nodded as he returned the repeating rifle to its boot. "In that case," he said, patting the book in his pocket, "I'd best get to studying, so we'll be ready for it. Sure as hell don't wanna end up like these poor folks."

The two men stared uneasily at the tomb of a church for a long moment. Then they mounted their animals and, riding through the necropolis that was once Piedras Negras, headed for the muddy channel of the Rio Grande and the providence of Texas beyond.

Chapter Three

The Sierra Diablo Mountains, Texas
April 1870

For over a month's time, Dead-Eye and Job rode the deserts of West Texas, attempting to determine which direction would set them firmly back on the trail of Jules Holland and his band of otherworldly outlaws. Several times, Brimstone sensed traces of the marauders' demonic steeds, but lost them almost as quickly. If the renegade vampire and the dark enchantress Evangeline had traveled that way before them, it had been months or perhaps even a year ago.

The chill of winter soon gave way to the heightening heat of spring. As the two headed northward, they found themselves approaching the mountainous range of the Sierra Diablo. They departed the level plain of scrub grass, cactus, and yucca, then slowly ascended the sloping steppes of the creosote flats. Soon, they found themselves traveling within a labyrinth of sandstone canyons. Tall cliffs of sedimentary rock rose around them, many bearing the ancient drawings of long bygone civilizations.

The desert wind whistled mournfully through the narrow ravines and, every now and then, they caught sight of a striped lizard sunning on a shelf of shale, a skittish jackrabbit on the run, or a black crow appraising them from a crest of stone. When Job saw such a dark bird, he couldn't help but think of his witch of a daughter and wonder if she was watching their progress through the raven's beady eyes.

On the second night of their journey through the mountains, the two sat around a campfire, each occupied with their own thoughts and chores. Dead-Eye disassembled the nickel-plated Dragoon, oiling the gun and checking its loads, then serviced the Belgium-made shotgun as well. The sawed-down barrels of Damacus steel gleamed in the flickering light as he worked. Job smoked his pipe and studied the little book of voodoo spells and incantations. As he had said before, he knew it would be wise to study up on its contents as much as possible, in order to counter or defeat any otherworldly menace that may be pitted against them.

The little black man was filling the bowl of his pipe with a second charge of tobacco when he looked across the fire and found the gunfighter staring at him. "So, what's on your worm-eaten brain this evening?" He had ridden with the dead man long enough to know when he was itching to ask a question, usually one that annoyed or vexed the Louisiana mojo man to no end.

"Just wondering if you've given it any further thought?" Dead-Eye replied, returning the big .44 pistol to the cross-draw holster that angled across his belly.

"And what exactly would that be?" Job acted oblivious, although he had a fair idea what the tall Southerner was referring to.

"Whether we should use that talisman," he countered. "The one your pappy gave you back at Black Bayou."

Job relit his pipe, drew in a lungful of smoke, then expelled it through his nostrils with a long sigh. He reached into one of the many pockets of his vest and withdrew a small object wrapped in white cloth. "You mean this?"

Dead-Eye nodded. "One and the same."

Carefully, as though handling a black widow spider instead of an inanimate object, Job unwrapped the item and held it aloft in the firelight. It was an amulet affixed to a golden chain interspersed with precious gems and black pearls. The talisman itself was the shape of an hourglass and fashioned from a pale blue stone of mysterious origin. A strange light seemed to pulse from within the center of the stone, shifting and swirling, almost hypnotic in nature.

"How many times have I told you?" Job asked him gravely. "The Stone of Kakudmi is not a thing to be trifled with. I'd not even have it in my possession, if my father hadn't insisted that I take it."

Dead-Eye seemed irritated by the negro's hesitation. "Just seems like we could save us a helluva lot of traveling and trouble if we'd simply use it. Send ourselves back in time, just before Jules Holland and the others took siege of my homestead in Georgia and turned my wife into a vampire and abducted my only son."

"And you're figuring we could prevail if we did so? Remember, we'd both return to the state of our former selves during that point in time.

Me woefully unprepared and you only a living mortal, without the ruthlessness or shooting skills my magic bestowed upon you following your resurrection from the dead. We'd just soon take a shaving razor and slit both our throats than face Holland and his gang the way we were four years ago. Besides, I'm not even certain both of us could use the talisman at the same time. There's no record of it ever having been employed in such a manner."

"We could give it a try," suggested the zombie. "Hightail it back to Washington town and stop that Booth feller from putting a bullet through President Lincoln's brainpan."

"I thought you were a supporter of the lost cause during the War Betwixt the States," Job said. "Didn't reckon you had such a great love for the bearded gentleman in the stovepipe hat."

"I've repented of my misguidance," Dead-Eye declared. "Besides, I just figured it might be a productive way of testing that confounded trinket, that's all."

"More than likely we'd end up ricocheting back and forth through eternity like my Papa did for nearly forty years." Job shook his head, wrapped the talisman in its cloth, and returned it to the pocket from where it had been stashed for safekeeping. "No, sir, you'd best get that damn fool notion plumb outta your head. I, for one, ain't about to put my trust in gris-gris that's caused such heartache and calamity."

"The time could come when you have no choice."

"Well, that time is a far piece off, in my opinion," Job told him flatly. "Now I'm aiming to settle down and get some shut-eye. You can sit here and tend the fire, or stare into oblivion, or whatever the hell you do when other folks are sleeping."

Dead-Eye frowned and grunted in resignation, aware that his suggestion had fallen on deaf ears. "Don't expect me to move a muscle if I spy a scorpion or sidewinder crawling into your blankets, you cantankerous old jaybird. I'll give them my blessing and say, 'Have at it'."

Job's precious metal grin twinkled in the light of the fire. "Believe you me, I'd prefer their company over your contrary, flyblown ass any ol' day or night." Then he burrowed beneath the woolen covers, tipped his bowler over his eyes, and was snoring in less than a minute's time.

"I smell death," said Job as they rode through a narrow pass the following afternoon. He lifted his eyes to a dozen buzzards perched upon craggy outcroppings along the canyon walls. "So, why are the scavengers roosting, rather than feasting?"

"I reckon 'cause there's not much left to feast upon," replied Dead-Eye as they rode closer to the scene of carnage.

Scattered across the rocky floor of the canyon was a multitude of bones. From the looks of them, they appeared to belong to three men and three horses. There was also a smaller heap that looked to have been a pronghorn deer—probably the prize of the others' hunt—before disaster befell them.

The two men swung down from their saddles and walked over to the skeletal remains. They were surprised to see that the bones had been stripped clean of meat, hide, and hair. Not a bit had been left behind.

"Something devoured them," the gunfighter said grimly. He shucked his .44 from its holster and held it at his side. "Something with an all-powerful hunger. And it sure as hell wasn't a wake of buzzards that did it." He looked up at the dark birds. They stared at the floor of the canyon balefully, more than a little peeved and disappointed that there was nary a speck of tissue or flesh left to harvest.

The mojo man knelt and examined a man's femur. The surface of the bone was scored and scarred with small bite marks. "Well, it wasn't something large, such as a cougar or bear, or even a pack of coyotes. The critters that did this were likely the size of a ground hog or smaller."

Dead-Eye grimaced and laid his thumb across the spur of the Dragoon's hammer, ready to cock and fire. "Whatever they were, they had a voracious appetite like nothing I've ever come across. Do you reckon it was another monstrosity unleased from the Hole Out of Nowhere?"

Before Job could answer, the albino mule named Balaam snorted nervously from his nostrils. In turn, Brimstone whinnied and tossed his black-maned head. The two men lifted their eyes, focusing their attention on the mouth of the pass ahead of them, as well as the direction they had traveled only a few moments before.

Men on horseback blocked the mountain canyon on both ends, perhaps seven or eight in each party. Their hair was long and pitch black, and their skin deep bronze in color, both traits of their native heritage. They wore long-sleeved, collarless shirts, cotton britches, and knee-high boots, some of them belonging to fallen cavalrymen. A few shouldered bows and quivers of arrows, as well as long-bladed knives sheathed on their belts. However, most toted longarms—Springfield rifles and military repeaters.

The ball of Dead-Eye's thumb itched to cock his piece. "Indians," he said beneath his breath.

Job's eyes narrowed as he studied those who surrounded them. "Apache, if I were to make an educated guess."

"I've heard they're a ruthless bunch. We could end up liberated of our scalps or buried to the neck in an anthill."

The mojo man regarded his companion with a sideward glance. "Don't go flying off the handle now. True, we've heard tales of how hostile the Apache have been in this territory, but we're not certain of their intentions, so let's just stay calm and hear them out."

A short, broad-faced man on a speckled Appaloosa broke away from the gathering at the eastern mouth of the pass and rode slowly toward them. His eyes were as dark and cold as the blued steel of the Spencer rifle he held, muzzle skyward, in his right hand. Job and Dead-Eye attempted to read the emotion that lay in those steely orbs, but found it difficult to do so.

"Fear not," the man told them as he stopped and dismounted on the far side of the field of bones. "We have no quarrel with the dark-skinned man. And we are respectful of the dead." He looked from the scattering of denuded bones to the tall Southerner in the black broadcloth suit. "That which lays fallow upon the earth, as well as those who walk among the living."

"I am Job," the negro said in introduction, "and this here's..."

"The one called Dead-Eye," replied the man with a nod. "I have heard of you both. I am Victorio."

Job removed his derby hat out of respect. "We have heard of you also. A great warrior and chieftain of the Chiricahua."

Victorio smiled bitterly. "Also a renegade, murderer, and thief, if you believe the tales of the white man's tongue. Those across the border have made that claim as well."

"I neither believe nor disbelieve those tales," Job told him firmly. "If they are true, I suppose you had good reason for what you've done."

"Perhaps." Victorio lowered the muzzle of his repeating rifle and pointed it to the bones upon the ground. "Tell me, what do you make of this?"

"Whoever they were, they put up a hellacious fight... and were dismally defeated."

"They were three of my best hunters and most fierce warriors," the

Apache told him. "My heart would not be so unsettled if they had fought mortal men and died with courage in battle. However, their blood screams out to me in terror and their bones, broken and gnawed, speak of some great and horrible evil."

"I'm of the same inclination," said the mojo man. "Never have I seen evidence of such a ravenous hunger. And surely not from a creature of this world."

It was at that moment that the gathering of men at the eastern mouth of the pass parted and a woman on a chestnut mare emerged into view. She sat tall in the saddle, darkly beautiful, yet solemn of countenance. She was adorned in a beaded tunic and vestments of fringed buckskin and held a long staff in one hand. It was embellished with bones, feathers, and shards of polished quartz and amethyst, and mounted at the pinnacle was the painted skull of a crow.

"Lozen seeks council with you," Victorio told him. "She says that you are a man of strong medicine. A shaman from dark waters. Is this true?"

"Yes," admitted Job. "And who might she be?"

"Lozen is my sister," said the Apache chief . "She is my right hand... strong as a man, braver than most, and cunning in strategy. Lozen is a shield to her people... a prophetess and healer. That is why she seeks your advice."

"Then she shall have it."

Victorio nodded respectfully, then turned his horse back in the direction of the others. Without hesitation, Job and Dead-Eye mounted Balaam and Brimstone respectively and followed.

As they joined the party of Apache braves, Job looked back and saw the second party approach the scene of merciless slaughter. They appraised the fleshless bones of their brethren for a reverent moment, then dismounted and began to gently gather them for ceremonial burial, leaving the remains of the animals behind.

Chapter Four

Victorio's Encampment
April 1870

For nearly an hour's time, they ascended the mountain range until they reached a natural mesa between two of the highest peaks in the Sierra Diablo. There, upon the flat of the plateau, was Victorio's stronghold.

Dead-Eye and Job were surprised to find the place to be more of a village than a hideout common to outlaws and those running from the law. There were eight wickiups constructed of bowed branches and mud in a half-circle, and, in the center of them, a lodge house covered with painted hides. A few yards away was a corral with two dozen fresh horses. All bore the brands of a number of ranches in the area, as well as the U.S. Army.

The women of the camp regarded the two visitors as they rode in with the others, not with fear, but interest. They knew that their leader would not have shared the secrecy of their location if they hadn't gained Victorio's trust. The children of the tribe eyed Dead-Eye with a mixture of apprehension and awe. The lanky gunfighter was a head taller than most of the braves of the tribe and his stoic, sunken face and glowing left eye, as well as the big Dragoon pistol holstered across his lean belly, was surely a sight for their young eyes to behold.

After dismounting and handing the reins of her mare to a young boy, the woman named Lozen beckoned for Job and Dead-Eye to follow. Soon, they were sitting around a small fire within the lodge of hides. It was dark inside the structure and the air smelled of woodsmoke, incense, and dried medicinal root. The only ones allowed inside the lodge were the Apache woman, her brother, and their two visitors.

"My people are in grave danger," Lozen told them. "They dwell in the shadow of an evil that once plagued the Apache in the days of our forefathers."

"Does this evil have anything to do with the carnage we came across back in that mountain canyon?" asked Job.

"It does." The woman opened a wicker basket beside her and withdrew an object. She handed it across the fire to the mojo man.

It was a swath of animal hide, perhaps antelope or deer. In the center of the skin was a drawing that was fading with age. It depicted a great, yellow beast being attacked by a pack of tiny, black creatures. Their sharp fangs tore into the belly of the behemoth, ripping it asunder and devouring the animal's pale entrails.

"What is this?"

"Our grandfather, Chato, was a shaman. He inscribed this from a vision that came to him following an attack on his village long ago. An attack that slaughtered his tribe and nearly cost him his life."

Dead-Eye took the scrap of hide and studied it. "Are you saying that your grandpappy's village was set upon by these ugly, little critters?"

"Yes. They are of ancient legend, not only for our tribe, but others as well. Those in Mexico call them *diablos hoyos*. Devils from the pit of Hell. They are commanded by the being known as Gaan, the Fallen One, and said to possess a hunger that cannot be appeased. They will bring down any living thing in their path and strip it of its flesh and bowels. Only the bones of those they slay are left behind, as testament to their fury."

"And you believe these pit-devils have returned?" Job asked.

"Those you discovered in the canyon were not the first to die," said Victorio. "A woman and child from our camp were attacked by the devils at a waterhole a short walk from here. The boy's skull was found intact, but his bones had been shattered and the marrow sucked away and consumed. Also, there is a town six miles southeast of the mountains named Sulfur Springs. There is a livery stable at the edge of the settlement and six horses were set upon and devoured in the dead of night. The devils took them swiftly and silently. The townspeople had no knowledge of the attack until early the following morning."

"What about this yeller wildcat here?" Dead-Eye asked, pointing to the golden beast in the drawing. "How does it figure into all this?"

"I have no clue," Lozen said. "No creature like it has ever been seen in this region. I believe it is part of a prophecy our grandfather envisioned that has not yet come to be."

Job nodded and, taking the fragment of hide from the gunfighter, studied the painted image more closely. "These symbols etched around the border… some sort of incantation I would hazard to guess."

Lozen nodded. "They are words of thunder. Chato once spoke them to call forth the aid of the Great Spirit, Cochawa, to battle the black demons and drive them back to the pit from which they escaped." The woman closed her eyes and softly began to chant. "Ha-Nah… Putah-Hay… Shoh-Balah… Tra-Bow…." Before she could go any further, the sunlight beyond the lodge entrance dimmed with a gathering of storm clouds and a deep rumbling echoed in the distance.

"Words of thunder, indeed," said Job, impressed by the dark magic the chant had begun to conjure. "You spoke of a pit. Where would that be?"

"There is an arroyo a mile or so from the foothills. On its northern bank is an arch of stone and, in its shelter, a sulfur spring that widens into a vast pool. Two days ago, Victorio and his braves rode there to scout the place and see if it had been disturbed. It was. They say that a hole swirls within the churning waters… a pit of blackness that crackles with the blue fire of lightning around its edges."

Dead-Eye looked over at Job. "Sounds like the Hole Out of Nowhere."

Job nodded. "Or a portal much like it." The negro regarded the Apache woman. "Any idea how this hole in the pool came about?"

"Many believe the scourge of black devils came after strangers rode through this territory thirteen moons ago," said Victorio. "The man known as The One Who Feasts on Blood and his three desperados."

A dark expression crossed the lovely face of Lozen. "And, with them, the Woman of Endless Shadow."

Job and Dead-Eye looked at one another. *Evangeline*, both thought, but dared not say the name aloud. If Victorio and his followers were aware that the dark enchantress had unleashed the pit-devils purposely, more than likely as a hindrance to slow the gunfighter and mojo man's pursuit, the Apache tribe's hospitality might very well be short-lived.

"If you can drive the demons back into the sulfur pit with your grandfather's incantation, why do you seek my help?" Job asked the woman across the fire.

"Once they are back in the chasm they sprang from, the opening must be sealed shut," Lozen told him. "I do not possess the magic to do so. My hope was that you did."

"I've closed such thresholds before," admitted the swamp sorcerer. Job ignored the look Dead-Eye was giving him at that moment. "If it's within my power, I'll surely do my best to close this one."

Lozen's face grew troubled. "Another thing… last night Chato came to me in a dream. He sat across the fire in the place you sit now. He was silent, but his eyes warned me of woeful misfortune. Outside the lodge, I could hear the screams of my people and the snarling of many beasts. I believe this was an omen of forthcoming tragedy. I am convinced the devils will attack this village soon. Perhaps even tonight."

"Then we'd best put our heads together and be ready for them," Job told her.

The woman regarded Dead-Eye. "I sense that the black steed you ride holds a presence that is not of this world. Perhaps that could be a strength in our favor."

"Despite his hellish disposition, Ol' Brimstone is loyal and ready to do what needs to be done," the gunfighter assured her. "We'll herd those little bastards back to the purgatory they sprang from, while you and Job tend to the dark magic and witchery."

"The devils only hunt at night," Victorio told them. "Feast with us and rest, so that we may be ready for them when they attack."

"Let us see to our animals and we'll join you directly," Job told the man and his sister.

When the two were out of earshot of the lodge house, the tall Southerner voiced his displeasure. "Looks like we stepped smack dab into one helluva troublesome predicament. Been better if we'd crossed over these mountains and kept on riding."

"Considering that this 'troublesome predicament' more than likely came about because of us and those we pursue, I believe we owe it to these people to help defeat these creatures and set it right," Job said sternly.

"And another thing... what was all that about closing portals and such? I don't recollect that I've ever seen you open and close one under your own power."

"Fact of the matter is, I never have. But I wasn't about to admit that in their presence, not with that being the main reason we're still healthy and free of peril." He patted the leather book in his vest pocket. "I have been studying on it quite a bit lately, however, and believe I can do it when the time comes. Let me worry about performing my chore and you save your concerns for accomplishing your own."

"We'll get the job done," the dead man allowed. "I just don't cotton to the possibility of being stripped clean down to the bone in the process."

The little black man grinned slyly. "Those devils crave hot blood and warm flesh, so you shouldn't have anything to worry about. If they get a mouthful of your putrid ass, they'll spit you out and look for more appetizing vittles."

"Speaking of vittles, smells like they're cooking up your supper right now."

Job inhaled deeply and smiled. "Smells right appetizing. Wonder what's on the menu?"

Dead-Eye grinned and cocked his thumb toward a cookfire set up between two of the wickiups. Upon the framework of a spit, a large carcass roasted above the flames. "I've always heard tell that the Apache would just soon eat a horse than ride one."

Job was unperturbed. "Wouldn't be the first time for me, to tell the truth. I reckon I've consumed pert near anything that's flown, walked on four feet, or slithered on its belly." As they approached their own animals, he studied the coal black roan. Brimstone seemed pensive and aware of some impending danger that the white mule was oblivious to. "You know, I have an idea how we might just get the best of the evil that's coming for Victorio and his tribe."

"And what would that be?" asked the gunfighter.

"Perhaps the best way to fight a passel of demons is to challenge them with one of their own."

Chapter Five

The Devil's Arroyo
April 1870

It was shortly before midnight when the silence and solitude of the Sierra Diablo was invaded by death on the prowl.

A full moon cast a silvery glow across the peaks of the mountain range, as well as the floors of the canyons and narrow passes. The deep shadow that lay out of reach of the nocturnal glow suddenly came to life, growling, teaming with fury. Tiny fangs gnashed and sharp claws skittered against stone and earth as the darkness moved, en masse, from the foothills below and made its way up the winding maze of ravines toward the summit where the Apache camp stood dark and quiet.

As waves of black fury reached the mountain village, tiny eyes as bright as polished silver searched for evidence of those they had come to feast upon. They found the compound unoccupied, as well as an empty corral that possessed the lingering scent of horses. Half of the pack broke away from the others and stormed the dark wickiups as well as the larger structure of the lodge house. They emerged seconds later, frustrated, for the abodes of branches and sunbaked mud had been abandoned.

Ears pricked as the sound of a horse echoed from the far end of the village. Soon, they spotted a single animal—a coal-black roan—standing near a stand of jagged boulders. A collective hiss ran through the dark pack, followed by the throaty growl of unrestrained bloodlust. Then, as one, they surged toward their lone victim.

Twelve devils closest to the far perimeter of the camp staked their claim before the others could get there. They launched themselves upon the horse's neck and haunches, burying their fangs deeply into black hide and the muscle just beneath. But, before they could start ripping and tearing the steed apart, they sensed that something was frightfully wrong. A great swell of inner heat erupted from the wounds they had inflicted and they soon found their teeth charred to the roots and the pink flesh of their mouths and gullets scorched and scalded. Before they could disengage themselves, hellfire erupted from within the black horse, consuming coarse fur, from muzzle to tail. Shrieking in agony, they dropped from the animal's body, fully engulfed in flame. Several attempted to crawl away, but the roan's hooves rose and descended savagely, crushing them into smoldering puddles of cinder and ash.

The rest of the pack, however, refused to relinquish their prize. They surged forward, intent on overwhelming the animal and bringing it forcefully to the ground. But as they drew nearer, the black horse whirled to face them. Its dark eyes blazed brilliant red with an unholy glow and hot embers drifted from its flared nostrils as it snorted in contempt. Then it unleashed a thunderous howl that was more of Hell than horseflesh and from its open mouth shot a tongue of white-hot flame that washed across the first wave of attackers and completely consumed them, turning hair, flesh, and bone into a fine mist of disintegrating embers.

Before Brimstone could surge forward to charge the approaching creatures, Dead-Eye emerged from behind the boulders, hooked his boot into the stirrup at the horse's left side, and swung into the saddle. He drew the big .44 Dragoon from its holster and unleashed a volley of shots. Silver slugs found six of the dark demons and, upon contact, the critters burst into balls of sulfurous smoke and flame. The reaction of precious metal tunneling through the devils' bodies confirmed that they were fiends from some unholy realm.

A moment later, shrill war cries rang out and, from a neighboring pass, emerged Victorio and ten of his men on horseback. They galloped toward the milling pack of pit-devils, firing their rifles as they rode. Several of the creatures exploded as silver pierced them. Dead-Eye nodded in approval.

At first he had thought it futile when Job had substituted the slugs from their cartridges with bullets he had cast from melted silverware, but he now saw that the effort had paid off.

Four devils emerged from behind the lodge house to their right, snarling savagely as they launched themselves at two of the Apache on horseback. The braves cried out in alarm as they were knocked bodily from their saddles. They hit the earth hard, attempting to fight off the black demons that had latched onto them. One died almost instantly, the fangs of a devil biting through the flesh of his throat, ripping past muscle and gullet, nearly decapitating the Indian. The second devil wrenched at his belly, shredding the muscles of his abdomen and burrowing deeply into the gory pit of his innards.

Victorio leapt from his Appaloosa. Drawing a long-bladed knife from his belt, he attacked the devils, severing their heads from their spines. Then he went to work on the two that attacked the other brave. One of the demons snarled triumphantly and, with a yank of its powerful head, tore one of the man's biceps free from its moorings. However, before it could gobble down its trophy, the Apache chief drove the tip of the knife into its right eye socket. Honed steel sank deeply into its brain as Victorio bore down with all his might. As the fourth devil disengaged itself from the brave's thigh and scampered forward, the chief drew a Remington revolver from his waistband and blew away half of its skull.

"Let's herd these sons of bitches back the way they came," Dead-Eye called to the Apache leader. He unleashed twin shotgun blasts into the wave of beasts, then broke open the scattergun's breech and quickly reloaded.

Victorio helped the injured brave back into his saddle, then mounted his own horse. As he joined Dead-Eye, he surveyed the multitude of dark creatures milling around them. They had been leery of the demon horse and his hellish fury at first, but gradually their nerve returned and they began to inch slowly toward them. "How many do you think there are?"

"Three dozen, more than likely," the gunfighter told him. His glowing left eye cast a pale luminance over the fore ranks of the pack. The beasts' tiny faces, eyes gleaming angrily and fangs gnashing hungrily, no longer showed hesitation or fear. "Maybe more. I'd reckon it's about time for your sister to do her part. I'd say we're less than a half minute away from them charging and latching into us."

Victorio raised his hands to his mouth and unleashed a cry like the shriek of an eagle. Almost immediately, the voice of Lozen responded from the ledge of a distant bluff. Melodically, she began to chant the ancient words of her shaman grandfather.

"Ha-Nah... Putah-Hay... Shoh-Balah... Tra-Bow..."

Lozen's invocation echoed off the sheer walls of the surrounding canyons, rising upward toward the heavens. Above them, a sky that had once been clear and filled with a billion stars abruptly began to darken and grow surly with gathering storm clouds. Thunder rolled deeply, reverberating through the night air, causing the earth beneath them to tremble.

"Mahola... Nan-Doha... Jee-Mohah... Fra-Bra-Ohey..."

Slowly, a heaviness filled the air, thick with the smell of approaching rain. Thunder rumbled again and, a moment afterward, a whipcrack of lightning pierced the clouds. The jagged finger of raw power hit earth between the army of demons and Dead-Eye and the others. Half a dozen of the beasts were blinded and scorched by the heavenly strike. Frightened, the rest lost their resolve, then swiftly turned tail and ran back down the narrow pass from where they had emerged.

"Alright, we've got 'em on the run!" Dead-Eye yelled out. "Let's go!"

As Brimstone galloped forward, a couple of stubborn pit-devils held their ground and snapped their wicked jaws sharply in defiance. The black horse's glowing eyes narrowed as he expelled another burst of demon fire from his gullet. The wave of flame consumed the rebellious pair where they stood.

Surging forward, the Morgan took chase. The zombie gunfighter allowed his horse to take the lead and began to reload his long-barreled Colt with powder, silver slugs, and percussion caps. The act was tedious by nature, but nearly impossible while on horseback. Soon, however, he had the big Dragoon fully loaded and primed. *The next town we come to, I'm gonna have this blasted hogleg retooled for newfangled cartridges!* he promised himself.

Job and Lozen sat atop their mounts on the edge of the cliff and watched the dark wave of flesh-eating abominations surge down the narrow pass beneath them. A moment later, Dead-Eye, Victorio, and the braves followed, firing their guns at the retreating devils. The storm overhead built in intensity, crashing and rumbling so tempestuously that the reports of the pistols and rifles were swallowed by its heavenly fury.

"Time to join them!" Job called out loudly. He spurred Balaam in the flanks, sending the snow-white mule down a narrow trail that lead to the canyon floor. Lozen nodded, but dared not answer. Urging her chestnut to follow, she continued to chant the incantation Chato had inscribed upon the sacred scroll of painted hide, calling upon the Great Spirit, Cochawa, to unleash retribution upon those his foe, the Fallen One, had unleashed from the boiling pit of the Devil's Arroyo.

Several minutes later, the two caught up to the others.

"What took you so long?" Dead-Eye hollered over the fury of the storm as Job pulled his white mule even with the black horse.

"Like I said before, you worry about doing your part and I'll do the same," the mojo man told him. Then, amid the tribe of Apache riders, they continued through the mazework of narrow canyons with only the benefit of heavenly lightning overhead to guide their way.

Eventually, they reached the foothills and the flat of the Texas desert beyond. Spurred by Lozen's reciting of Chato's chant and the maelstrom it conjured, the tiny, black beasts swarmed across the barren land. A particularly brilliant thunderbolt revealed the multitude of snapping, snarling fury that fled ahead of them. Where they had once thought there to be only three or four dozen of the pit-devils, the lightning flash showed there to be a hundred or more.

Job looked over and sensed that Lozen was struggling. Her voice began to grow hoarse and weary, for she had been chanting for nearly an hour since she first began on the ledge above the Apache stronghold. The mojo man had heard enough during the ride to memorize the incantation, so he took up the slack and began to loudly chant the words himself. Lozen regarded him thankfully as her voice cracked and gave out. The heavens continued to rumble and spit jagged fingers of blue electricity as the Apache prophetess surrendered the ancient ritual to the black sorcerer she had placed her trust in.

Suddenly, a lightning flash revealed a great arch of red stone in the distance. "There!" shouted Victorio. "The Devil's Arroyo!"

The crackle of heavenly fire descended, striking above the deluge of dark beasts… searing their fur and scorching the flesh of their backs. Most ran onward, shrieking, toward the place of their origin, fully engulfed in flame. But a dozen or more grew defiant as they neared the arroyo and its sulfur pool. They whirled and faced their pursuers, prepared to launch into them and fight to the death. Dead-Eye, Job, and the others refused to give ground, however. The riders surged forward, firing into the milling wave of beasts. Silver slugs burrowed through hair and flesh, violating their evil essence and causing them to burst into fireballs of unholy combustion. Several dived toward the horses' ankles, but Brimstone and Balaam fended them off—the black roan with a burst of hellfire from between glowing, red teeth and the albino mule with flashing silver horseshoes.

Soon, the sandstone arch loomed near and Lozen spurred her chestnut mare forward. As she passed, Job heard her continuing the chant, her voice rested and restored. Shouting to the turbulent heavens, the Apache woman skirted the outer boundary of the fleeing herd, intending to reach the arroyo before them.

"Ha-Nah... Putah-Hay... Shoh-Balah... Tra-Bow..."

As the storm began to reach its pinnacle, the nocturnal posse watched from horseback as Lozen leapt from her saddle and shimmied up the precarious bow of the arch. A minute later, she was standing at its peak, arms raised skyward. Even through the crash of thunder and lightning, they could hear her voice reciting the chant at a fevered pitch. A strong gale joined the tempest, rushing across the plains, churning up dust and pebbles amid its current. The horses of Victorio's tribe struggled to retain their footing, while several of their riders were thrown from their saddles by the force of the squall. As Dead-Eye and Job reached the stone arch, the last of the pit-devils reached the edge of the sulfur spring. The creatures plunged into the boiling waters and swam toward the unearthly portal that spun and crackled in the center of the pool.

"Best get to closing that hole!" Dead-Eye hollered over the roar of the gale.

Taking the little, leatherbound book from his vest pocket, Job swung down off Baalam and, fighting against the wind, struggled to make his way to the edge of the pool. "That's what I'm aiming to do... if I don't get knocked on my ass first!"

When the final demon had made its escape into the portal, Job sensed that the fury of the storm was beginning to abate. He looked up to see Lozen standing atop the crest of the sandstone arch. The Apache woman had ended the incantation of her ancestor Chato. Solemnly, she stared down at the negro and nodded. She had accomplished what she had set out to do. Now it was his turn.

The mojo man cracked open his book and scanned a yellowed page that he had studied diligently over the past few months. He reached to his necklace of charms and gris-gris, grabbed a tiny, blue-glassed bottle between his dark fingers, and yanked it free. He then crushed the container within his grasp and flung a cloud of equally blue powder upon the roiling currents of the hot spring. The powder expanded and traveled toward the center of the pool, where the portal lay. It reached the sparkling edges of the otherworldly threshold and remained there.

Job began to recite an incantation written in his book of spells and moved his free hand in a series of circular and triangular gestures. His eyes were locked on the portal and, at first, he was afraid that the magic he was conjuring was having no effect. Then, gradually, the border of the dark hole in the pool began to shrink and close in on itself.

When the portal reached half its circumference, Job saw something stir within the darkness beyond the gateway. It was similar to the leering faces of the black-bristled pit-devils, but its glowing countenance was much more contorted and terrifying. The monstrosity began to rise toward the opening, fangs bared and its massive eyes burning like fiery coals.

The Fallen One! thought Job, recalling the ancient Apache legend. Part of him wanted to turn and flee in terror, but another part knew that he had a job to complete. If he didn't, the true source of the flesh-eating critters would escape and be unleashed upon them all. Determined to make sure that didn't happen, he began to increase the speed of the gestures and give more force and fortitude to the words of the spell he recited.

All watched as the portal began to recede, shrinking to the dimension of a wagon wheel, then the size of a cast-iron skillet. Just before the opening closed with a bullwhip *crack*, one of the demon's hellish eyes glared at them with contempt and defeat… then was gone.

Almost immediately, the desert night went silent. Lozen climbed down the slope of the arch and joined her brother and the others at the lip of the pool. The sulfurous water bubbled gently with no evidence that its surface had ever been corrupted by a gateway to another realm.

As the storm clouds receded and disappeared, that night's moon cast a pale glow upon those gathered at the Devil's Arroyo. "Gaan and its underlings are gone," Lozen said with relief. She turned to Job and laid a hand on his shoulder in a gesture of respect. "Thank you. Your magic is strong and trustworthy. We were fortunate to have it with us this night."

The mojo man nodded and closed the leatherbound book. As he returned it to his vest pocket, he hoped the gloom hid the fact that his hands were trembling. "For the time being. But it will return someday… won't it?"

"Yes," said the Apache woman. "It will invade our world once again, to fulfill the prophecy of the Golden Beast. But not in our lifetime."

They stared at the sulfur spring for a moment longer, then walked to their mounts and prepared to return to Victorio's stronghold in the Sierra Diablos.

Dead-Eye and Job climbed atop Brimstone and Balaam, then followed behind the others.

"You accomplished a good night's work," the cadaverous gunfighter told his companion. "Hopefully it'll bring you a good night's sleep in return."

Job nodded. "More than likely. But all that riding fired up my appetite something fierce." He ran his tongue along his gold and silver teeth, dislodging a shred of meat. "If I'm lucky, there might be a bite or two more of that horse left over from supper."

Chapter Six

In the desert near Las Cruces
New Mexico Territory
Late July 1870

After bidding Victorio and Lozen farewell, Dead-Eye and Job left the barren range of the Sierra Diablo Mountains and rode northwestward.

As they neared the border leading to the New Mexico territory, they began to discover evidence of Holland and his entourage's passage through the region. Twenty miles past Fort Davis, they came across a stagecoach hitched to a team of four horses. From a distance, it simply seemed that they had stopped to allow the passengers a stretch of the legs and the animals a few minutes of much-needed rest. But as the two grew nearer, they discovered that their immobility had a more sinister explanation.

The coach, horses, driver and shotgun rider, and the passengers... all had been turned to stone. A couple of things suggested that their transformation had taken place during a robbery. One was the strongbox lying empty on the ground, while the other was the expressions of alarm on the faces of those staring from the windows of the coach's cabin.

Dead-Eye pulled Brimstone alongside the team's lead horse and laid a hand upon its left flank. The flesh and muscle were as smooth and hard as a marble tombstone. "I reckon there's nothing you can do to turn them back?" he asked the mojo man.

Job frowned. "Afraid not. It's like that preacher we came across back in Tennessee... the one who'd been changed into a pillar of salt. Whatever dark magic Evangeline is using to cast such spells of transformation, it's from some realm I'm completely ignorant of. And, if it's foreign to the teachings I've learnt from my papa or this here book in my pocket, then there's not a damn thing I can do about it."

They came across more devilry in the cattle town of Van Horn. They were buying supplies at the mercantile, when four ranchers approached them, having heard tales of Dead-Eye's and Job's past dealings with the supernatural. It seemed that a number of their longhorn cattle had contracted vampirism after Jules Holland and his gang had ridden through nearly a year before. The bloodthirsty herd—totaling nearly sixty in all—terrorized the town and surrounding territory in the dead of night. A fee of a thousand dollars was negotiated before the two agreed to take on the task.

For nearly a month, a hunting party led by the zombie gunfighter and the mojo man rode the flatlands from sundown to daybreak. One by one, they hunted down the undead cattle, roping and tying them, then driving sharpened stakes the size of fence posts through their hearts. It was when the number destroyed reached well past eighty head that they realized that the herd had been feeding upon and cursing cattle from other ranches far beyond their area. Aware that the task could possibly last for months, perhaps even years, Job left the ranchers with the knowledge and weapons necessary to combat the blood-sucking cows, then they collected their wages and finally continued on their way.

It was midway through summer when the two finally crossed from the state of Texas into the desert wilderness of the New Mexico territory.

For several days they rode across the arid plains with a relentless sun blazing down upon them throughout the day. At night, the flatland of scrub brush, mesquite, and tall boulders grew cool beneath a canopy of limitless stars. Often, Job would lay in his blankets and point out the various constellations, much to Dead-Eye's exasperation.

"Yonder is Equuleus the Horse and Gemini the Twins. Then, toward the north is Lyra the Harp. Further west there's Serpens the Snake."

Dead-Eye picked a few maggots from his mustache and eyed the night sky himself. "You missed one," he said, leveling a shriveled finger at a cluster of stars. "The Drunken Cowboy in the Washtub with the Long-Legged Whore."

"Mock me if you wish," grumbled the negro. "Just trying to impart some much-needed education on your ignorant ass with my expertise of astronomy and such."

"Oh, you mean like Ursa Major the Great Bear or Vulpecula the Fox," retorted the gunslinger with a grin. "Or maybe Cassiopeia the Mother of Andromeda hanging right over that billiard ball-sized head of yours."

Miffed, Job cocked his derby hat over his eyes with a huff. "Enough of this nonsense! Stop your caterwauling and let me get some sleep!"

On their fifth day, as they neared the jagged granite peaks of the Organ Mountains, they spotted a dark structure of some sort abandoned a half-mile away. As they approached with caution, they discovered that it was the remains of a Conestoga wagon. The prairie schooner's team had been cut loose from the tongue and stolen, then the wagon itself had been set on fire. Only the frame, wheels, and tent hoops remained, charred black and still smoldering in places.

"Looks like someone crossed paths with misfortune," said Dead-Eye grimly. "Think it was Indians or outlaws?"

Job slipped down from his white mule and studied a multitude of tracks around the wagon. "Mostly Pueblo dwell hereabouts, but they're peaceful for the most part," he said. "The shoes of these horses were forged and shod by a blacksmith, and a skillful one at that. I'd say some cruel hombres attacked this family without warning. Don't see any rifle casings lying about to signify a gunbattle of any kind."

Dead-Eye was climbing down from his black roan, when a faint creak came from the front of the wagon. The gunfighter drew his .44 from its holster and nodded toward the forward wheels. *There's someone underneath,* his eyes warned. Job nodded silently and shucked the brass-framed Henry from its saddle boot.

Quietly, Dead-Eye made his way down the length of the wagon and paused for a long moment. He could hear excited breathing from the space between the scorched driver's seat and the axle. The gunfighter cocked his pistol, then slowly crouched and peeked beneath the body of the carriage.

What he found there was exactly what he *hadn't* expected to find. A small girl, perhaps six years old, perched bird-like atop the shaft of the front axle. Her face and clothing were dirty and grease-stained, and her bright blue eyes gleamed not with fright, but menace.

Dead-Eye grunted in surprise. "What in tarnation?"

Abruptly, the crack of a gunshot sounded and the Southerner rocked backward on his heels as something slammed forcefully into his forehead. He landed on his ass in the dirt, addled for an instant.

Job jacked the lever of the repeating rifle. "Whoever's under there, come on out. We're here to help, not to cause harm. Looks like there's been enough of that done already."

A moment later, the child crawled into the open. She stood, scarcely as tall as the mojo man's hip, all curly blonde hair and freckled face. She held a single-shot Derringer in her right hand. They expected the girl to be scared half out of her wits, but instead she seemed perplexed and downright peeved.

"Why ain't you lying stone-cold dead?" she asked the tall man in the black broadcloth suit. "I shot you square betwixt the eyes!"

Dead-Eye reached up and probed at the bullet hole two inches above the bridge of his nose. "Sorry to disappoint you but, believe it or not, this isn't the first time I've had my brains blown out," he told her. "It was a damn good shot, though. You oughta be proud."

The girl stuck the little pistol in her apron pocket and planted both hands on her hips. She eyed Job suspiciously. "Well, if this don't beat all! It's plain to see that this fella is buzzard food. So how is it he's still breathing and talking?"

"Well, to tell the truth, he ain't precisely breathing anymore," the negro explained. "As for the talking, he does a sight more of it than I can stomach sometimes." He studied her with concern. "Child, what happened here?"

The girl's bravado slipped a notch or two. "We were on our way from El Paso to my grandfolks' place in the Arizona territory... a town called Holbrook. We made it this far and was set upon by a gang of no-account, lowdown sons of bitches... thirteen of them in all. Called themselves Baker's Dozen on account they were led by a one-armed man named Otis Baker. They called out to us all friendly-like, but Ma and Pa were never overly trusting of strangers. Before they rode into camp, they made me hide in the tact box, so those fellas never even knew I was there."

Dead-Eye regained his feet and dusted off the seat of his britches with his hat. "Where's your folks at now, girl?"

The child's eyes burned hot with rage, but soon tears bloomed and ran down her filthy cheeks in rivulets. "I watched from a crack beneath the lid of the box. When they caught sight of Ma and my elder sister, Rebecca, those men got a nasty look on their faces. That's when all hell broke loose. They drew their guns and marched Pa, Ma, and Becky beyond that cluster of rocks yonder. There was a gunshot, then crying and screaming from my mother and sister." The girl stared at the ground, her tiny hands balled tightly. "It went on for an awful long time. Then two more shots and I could hear those men coming back toward the wagon. I crawled out of the tact box and hid yonder behind a clump of cactus. They cut Pa's team of mules loose, looted the wagon of supplies, then Otis Baker doused it with liquor from his saddle bag and set it aflame. After that, they skedaddled."

"What's your name, child?"

"Melissa Mae Slatter," she told him. "But my folks just call me Missy… or they used to." She studied the two curiously. "Who are you?"

"I'm Job, like that boil-infested gent in the Bible. And this here's Dead-Eye. How long have you been out here by yourself?"

"Nigh onto four days now," Missy replied. "I took me a tin of hardtack and a canteen with me when I snuck away from the wagon, but that's all gone now. I'm mighty famished and parched, to tell the truth."

Job took the girl by the hand and led her toward the white mule and the canvas packs that hung across its flanks. "Well now, we can take care of that right here and now." As he ushered the girl toward Baalam, the black man locked eyes with Dead-Eye. The gunfighter nodded solemnly, then turned and walked toward the mass of boulders the girl had mentioned before.

After feeding Missy beef jerky, leftover cornbread, and canteen water, Job left her sitting in the shade of a mesquite tree and met Dead-Eye as he returned to the burnt-out wagon. "Well?"

"It's a sorry sight," the zombie told him in a low voice. "Her pa was forced to kneel, then was shot in the back of the skull. After that, well… her ma and sis were violated and killed. It didn't go fast or easy." The muscles of the gunfighter's jaw clenched tightly and his right eye, as gray as gunmetal, burned with a dark contempt that Job was well acquainted with. "I'm thinking if they'd known Lil' Miss was there, they would've captured and taken her to sell… or else subjected her to the same fate as her kin."

"I reckon it's up to us to see that she gets safely to her grandparents," Job said softly. "We'll take her to the next town, put her up in a hotel, and telegraph her grandparents to come get her."

Dead-Eye shook his head stubbornly. "No, sir. I aim to deliver her into their hands myself. A child like that has no more business being left stranded in a strange town than abandoned in the middle of the desert like she was." He walked over to Baalam and dug through one of the canvas packs until he found a shovel. "I'm gonna get to work digging some graves for those poor folks."

"You can give Ma and Becky a proper burial," said a small voice. "But we'll be taking Pa with us."

Both men turned to find Missy Slatter standing no more than six feet behind them.

"Just how much of what we said did you overhear, Lil' Miss?" asked Dead-Eye.

"All of it. Ma always said I had more ears than a field of corn and enough mouth to preach Old Scratch into baptism."

"I'll not argue that point with you," said Job. "And what's this about not burying your papa?"

"Pa was a hard-working man and God-fearing, although not as much as Ma," the child explained. "He never wanted for much, but he made one thing mighty clear. If he should up and kick the bucket, he wanted his body laid to rest in the family cemetery where he grew up. I suppose we should grant him that wish at least, don't you think?"

The mojo man crouched and laid gentle hands on the girl's shoulders. "Missy, we'll be riding a long while through the hot desert in the middle of summer. In that kind of heat, your father's body will turn awful ripe after a while."

Missy's eyes turned to the tall Southerner holding the spade. "Well, he can't be any more stinky or dead than this feller standing right here, now can he?"

The zombie grinned and chuckled. "Nothing gets past you, does it, gal?"

Job scratched his stubbled chin in consideration. "I suppose I could cast a spell of preservation on him like I did this fly-blown feller here. It won't last forever, but it should help."

"Don't worry, Lil' Miss," Dead-Eye assured her. "I'll bury your ma and sister, then I'll bundle up your papa and lash him across Brimstone's haunches. He ain't the type of horse that shies from toting his share of the dead."

The girl frowned regretfully. "I'm awful sorry that I shot you in the head, Mister Eye."

"Don't worry your pretty little head over that, child," he said with a wink. "If I'd been in your shoes, I'd done the same." Then, with the shovel canted over his shoulder, he headed off to do his digging.

Missy Slatter stared after him for a long moment. "He's nice, considering he's deceased and all. But sort of sad and moody, too."

Job smiled and shook his head. "Darling, you don't know the half of it." And, for the child's sake, he was content with leaving it that way.

Chapter Seven

Tulerosa
New Mexico Territory
August 1870

A week's traveling found them in the desert town of Tulerosa. They decided to lay over for a couple of days, to rest and take care of some overdue business.

Job's first stop was the telegraph office. He wired Missy's grandfather, Elmer Slatter of the town of Holbrook, and informed him of the deaths of his son, daughter-in-law, and teenaged granddaughter, as well as promised to bring young Missy to their Arizona homestead as soon as possible. Job knew that was bound to be another month or so, depending on what obstacles they might encounter along the way, but at least the young'un's grandparents knew she was safe and in friendly company until their reunion came to be.

Dead-Eye made good on his promise and sought out an apt gunsmith. He found one on Tulerosa's main street, a burly German by the name of Maximillian Eichhorst. The cadaverous gunfighter surrendered his Colt Dragoon for a day or so to be rechambered for modern .44-caliber cartridges and easier loading, rather than continuing to depend on the time-consuming practice of loading powder, lead, and percussion cap separately by hand. Eichhorst also agreed to load fifty cartridges with silver he would melt down from various objects Job had picked up along their journey.

As he turned to leave the gunsmith's shop, he noticed a counter of handmade knives. One, heavy and long-bladed with a hickory wood haft, caught his eye immediately. "It is one of a kind," the gunsmith told him. "Designed and made by Rezin Bowie himself. I bought it from a Mexican gentleman who said that he served under the command of Santa Anna. He claimed he took it off the body of Rezin's brother, Jim, following the siege of the Alamo in San Antonio. Whether that is the honest truth or a braggart's bunk, I cannot say. But it does have the initials JB carved into the handle just behind the guard, so it could very well be."

Dead-Eye hefted it in his right hand and found the big knife to be well-balanced. "I'll take it." He paid Eichhorst twenty dollars in gold coin for the weapon and a leather sheath to carry it in, which he hung from his belt on his left side, concealed beneath his frock coat.

Later that day, Job rolled his eyes when the tall Southerner showed off his new cutlery. "Now why the hell do you feel the need to tote something like that around when you have a big-ass cannon of a pistol and a sawed-off scattergun?"

Dead-Eye grinned slyly as he thought of the man named Garland Hughs, who he had left mutilated and staked to the earth for hungry buzzards in a Texas town with no name. "It'll come in handy next time I cross paths with some bastard worthy of a carving. Besides, I'll have my own and won't have need to borrow your little toenail-trimmer of a pig-sticker."

The following morning, Job was exiting a drinking establishment, where he had just finished an early hour libation or two, and discovered Missy Slatter running down the boardwalk toward him. The girl, dressed in a new blue calico dress and sunbonnet they had bought for her, seemed excited enough to bust.

"Lookee here, Mister Job!" she piped, waving something overhead. "Look what the nice feller with the medicine show wagon gave me! And it's all mine to keep!"

When the child reached him, the mojo man took the object and studied it. It was an oversized rectangle of weathered pasteboard, twice the size of a gambling card. On one side there was a black background of stars with a yellow crescent moon set in the center. The moon possessed a wicked face with a malevolent eye, a crooked nose, mustache, and chin whiskers. When he flipped the card over, he found an illustrated depiction of a young woman with a pageboy haircut, dressed in an outfit of chain mail and armor breastplate. She brandished a broadsword in one hand and a banner of white silk in the other. The military flag bore an image of Christ holding the world with an angel watching on each side, as well as the words *Jhesus Maria* embroidered in gold. The legendary Maiden of Orléans rode a white stallion, also outfitted for battle, and in the background was a turreted castle of gray stone.

"See?" said Missy happily. "It's Joan of Arc. That nice feller told me if I put it beneath my pillow when I sleep, I'll dream that I was her and fight valiantly in battle."

When the child reached up to retrieve her prize, the negro snatched it away. "Sorry to disappoint you, Missy, but it seems that I've come across such cards before. And, while it might seem like a magical toy to you, believe me, it most definitely isn't. Why, I'd just soon give you a basket full of rattlesnakes to play with than allow you to place this beneath your pillow tonight."

"I don't understand!" pouted the blond-haired child. Her face grew beet red and she looked on the verge of kicking Job in the shins with her new button-up boots. "How come I can't have it?"

"Just settle down and trust my judgment," he told her firmly. He reached into a vest pocket and withdrew several copper coins. "Here. Run over to the general store yonder and buy yourself some penny candy." *I'd rather you end up with rotten molars than get trapped in a corner of Hell I can't pry you out of,* he thought to himself.

"Awww, heck… okay!" Grudgingly, she took the money offered her and lit across the rutted dirt street to B. Jackson's Mercantile, her sweet tooth aching for jawbreakers, peppermint sticks, and horehound candy.

Job stood there for a moment and regarded the crowd that was beginning to disperse a couple of blocks down the street. With a scowl, he made his way down the boardwalk, intending to have a word or two with the fellow that Missy Slatter had encountered.

A moment later, he was standing before a brightly painted wagon with a team of two black horses tethered to the front. The elegantly-lettered words on the side of the cabin read DOCTOR AUGUSTUS LEECH'S TRAVELING MEDICINE SHOW—MAGIC, MUSIC, & MUSE—FEATURING THE GOOD DOCTOR'S PATENTED CURE-ALL ELIXIR!

The mojo man walked around to the back of the wagon, where the owner was busy loading the wares of his enterprise into the rear door of the cabin. He regarded the tall, thin man dressed in a long-tailed coat and stovepipe hat. Job glanced down at the back of the card in his hand and realized that the gaunt fellow's handlebar mustache and goatee were identical to the ones worn by the crescent moon.

"Pardon me," he said, after clearing his throat a couple of times.

The gaunt man turned and regarded the negro man with distaste. "Sorry. I only make my patented elixir available to folks of Caucasian heritage. I never peddle to redskins or nigg—"

Job leveled a dark finger at the medicine show man. "You allow that nasty word to slip past your lips and I'll curse you with a hellacious case of dysentery that'll keep you prisoner to the privy for a week or so."

The mustachioed gentleman regarded Job with amusement. "Oh, you believe you could do that, do you?"

"Not only do I believe, but I could make good on my threat if I had a mind to." He handed the oversized card to the fellow in the top hat. "I'm returning this to you. The child you gave it to has no need for it."

"Oh, you mean the little beauty with the hair spun of gold and eyes of bright azure," he said slyly. He looked down at the armored woman on the face of the card. "It was intended to be no more than a gift. A pleasant distraction in this hot and godforsaken place. Besides, the tot has been through so much heartache and trial as of late, I figured she was due some much-deserved escape from reality."

"As one of her temporary guardians, I reject the sort of escape that you propose," Job told him firmly. "I know what that card is and the place it opens doors to." He eyed the lanky man. "Tell me... would you be the same Doctor Augustus Leech that visited Bogalusa Parish in the heart of Louisiana in the year 1820? The one who peddled his evil concoction to the townsfolk and poisoned five adults and nine innocent children?"

"Really!" laughed the gentleman with a wolfish grin. "Do I appear to be that advanced in years?"

"Satan's minions often bargain for immortality. Besides, I never forget a face." Job dug through one of the many pockets of his vest and produced a yellowed card nearly identical to the one Missy Slatter had been given. This one, however, held the image of a fierce African Zulu warrior in war paint, brandishing an oval shield and ornate ceremonial spear. Contemptuously, he tossed the card at the entrepreneur's feet.

Augustus Leech bent down and retrieved the card. "Ah, yessss," he said softly, his voice like the seductive hissing of a serpent. "Young Job. Did you not take advantage of your gift and set out on the adventure that I offered you? Did you and your tribe not battle the colonizers and slave traders and parade proudly with their severed heads upon your spears?"

"I nearly did," Job admitted, "but my father was privy to your deception and the tragedy and terror it would bring. How many of your accursed dream cards did you hand out this afternoon?"

"Only one," said Leech. "To your freckle-faced young Missy. But I did sell nearly half a case of my elixir to a number of old ladies aching of arthritis and gout, as well as several young mothers in search of a cure-all tonic to sooth sick babies and alleviate the afflictions of their ailing youngsters."

Staring into the self-proclaimed doctor's dark eyes, Job felt as though he were standing toe to toe with the Devil himself. And, in a sense, he suspected he probably was. "I know the purpose of your confounded dream cards and your venomous elixir. Lucifer is a busy bastard, so he recruits agents to harvest the innocent and supply him with his quota of souls. I'm sure that you've gathered your fair share of them with your treachery and entrapment."

Leech closed the cabin's rear door, then walked past Job and climbed onto the seat of the wagon. "I'd love to continue this lively debate concerning my mission and your disdain for it, but I really must go. Like the Master, I am destined to roam to and fro, and up and down, this vast and untamed wilderness."

"And what about those you've peddled your poison to?" asked Job. "Shall they live or die?"

The medicine showman smiled and took the team's reins in hand. "I suppose that depends on your ability to locate those who made a purchase following my persuasive pitch and buy their treasured bottle of elixir back from them. I'm sure a few will do so for a few dollars more than I charged, but there are others who truly believe in the serum's virtues and shan't part with it for any price. They are the ones who have abandoned their trust in God and pledged their faith to Lucifer. It was a matter of their choosing, not yours or mine."

With that, Doctor Augustus Leech snapped the leather of the reins, sending the two black horses surging forward. It wasn't long until the garishly painted wagon and its black-clad occupant had moved far beyond the town limits of Tulerosa and disappeared amid the shimmering summer heat of the surrounding desert.

Job sighed and surveyed the busy town around him. When Leech had loaded the partial crate of his patented elixir into the back of the wagon, he noted that the container had originally contained thirty-six bottles. That meant that the crowd who had gathered to hear the soul-stealer's spiel had laid down money for eighteen bottles of the medicinal potion.

"Who was that feller you were talking to?" asked Dead-Eye, walking up to join him with little Missy tagging along behind.

"A bane of humanity and a burr in my ass," said the mojo man grimly. He took a bag of silver coins from his vest pocket, money intended for traveling expenses, but which now had a more consequential purpose. "Before we ride out, we've got a job to complete. And, considering we're strangers hereabouts, it may take some smooth-talking and sleight of hand to get it done."

The trio were two days back on the trail once again, when Dead-Eye found himself in the midst of a horrible nightmare. It was not one that was uncommon or comforting to him, that was for certain.

Somewhere his son cried out for him.

"Hush, child," said the voice of Evangeline. "Your father is dead."

But...but.. I'm not...

A tragic range of emotions flash through a man's mind at the point of death.

Sorrow.

Regret.

Loss.

And, sometimes, unbridled rage... at the injustice of it all.

"Daniel!" his father screamed. "I will come for you! I promise!"

Snake laughed. "Save your breath. Savor this moment... for it shall be your last." He took a step closer, bringing the gun within a foot of the man's face. "Tell my brethren in Purgatory that I said 'howdy.' They will torment you well."

The muzzle of the Remington yawned like the mouth of an empty cavern. But Joshua knew that was a lie. Something awaited him within. Something small and quick and cast of bad intent and wanton waste.

When the time of annihilation came in explosive powder, flame, and lead, the man named Joshua Wingade neither saw it nor felt it.

He simply failed to be.

Dead-Eye lurched from his fitful slumber with a muted cry. At first he was disoriented, unsure of his surroundings. Then his one good eye sought out points of reference, the moonlit backdrop of the San Andres Mountains to the northwest with its highest point, Salinas Peak, rising among them.

He looked over to where the little mojo man slept. Job snored loudly within the hollow of his derby hat, bundled tightly within his blankets like a papoose. It was chilly in the desert at night and the negro tended to complain of an aching in his bones the following morning if he failed to sleep warmly.

Dead-Eye reclined on the boulder he had been resting against and listened. From a distance, he heard the muffled sound of a child crying. He rose and walked to where Missy Slatter had made her place for the night. The blankets of her bedroll had been tossed aside and abandoned.

Without thinking, the gunfighter moved his hand toward the butt of his Dragoon pistol and found that it was gone. The holster was empty.

Instead, he drew the Bowie knife from its sheath and walked beyond the glow of the campfire to a scrubby stand of juniper. There, Brimstone and Balaam were tethered, and their burdens—canvas packs and the bundled body of the girl's father—lay on the ground nearby, until their departure the following day. He returned the dagger to its rightful place when he found the source of the weeping.

Missy sat crouched beside the body of her papa. Her head was bowed in defeat with both her small hands clutching the ivory grips of the big hogleg pistol. As Dead-Eye took a seat next to her, she whimpered and stared up at him. Her eyes were moist with tears and full of youthful rage.

"How can I face the men who killed my folks when the gun's too heavy for me to aim?" she asked angrily. "I can't even muster the strength to cock the hammer!"

Gently, Dead-Eye took the Dragoon from her grasp. "You were intending on leaving us and setting out on your own, were you?"

"I'm sorry I took your pistol," the girl apologized. "I was just borrowing, not stealing."

"I believe you," the Southerner assured her. "But a young'un your age has no business facing murderous desperados such as them."

Missy nodded glumly. "I know. But they can't just up and get away with it. Shooting Pa and doing Ma and Becky the way they did before killing them! What kind of justice is that?"

Dead-Eye sat there quietly for a long moment. "Lil' Miss?"

The girl scooted on her butt across the rocky earth and found comfort next to the dead man's side. "Yessir?"

"Do you believe in angels?"

Missy Slatter looked up at him, puzzled. "Sort of, I guess. My mother believed in them. Not sure that Pa or my sister did. Why do you ask?"

"Because I figure the Lord sends them to Earth to walk among us," he told her. "Some take care of you when you're sick or protect you during your travels. Then there's others that are given the task of setting things straight."

The child nodded. "You mean the avenging kind."

"Correct." The gunfighter felt along the ground until he located a jagged shard of flint. "You possess neither the strength nor skill for facing Baker's Dozen... but I do." He took the sharp edge of the stone and began to scratch something into the steel of the pistol's barrel. In the moonlight, the girl could see that it was a single word.

MISSY.

"I'm not claiming to be an angel or such. Far from it. But someday, God willing, I'll come across those sons of bitches that took your family from you and I'll act on your behalf," he promised, his mustachioed face solemn. "When I do, this will be *your* pistol, doing your bidding. I'll be the one who puts it to use… but only as a vessel for your desire and entitlement for vengeance."

Concern crossed the little girl's tear-streaked face. She reached out and took Dead-Eye's free hand. It was stiff and cold to the touch, but she held on tightly and did not pull her fingers away. "But there's an awful lot of 'em, Mister Eye. Thirteen in all."

Dead-Eye considered the nightmare he had relived a few minutes before. "My fear of death was stricken from me a long time ago. I shall face them for you, Lil' Miss. Bring down each and every one, and send them down the road to Hell they've paved for themselves."

"That's mighty big to offer, Mister Eye," Missy said with a yawn, "but I'm much obliged to you." A moment later she was fast asleep.

Dead-Eye carried the child back to camp and tenderly tucked her back into her woolen blankets. Afterward, he stood beside the fire and stared at the name he had inscribed on the barrel of the forty-four. Although he wasn't a religious man, he said a prayer for the orphaned girl. Then he holstered the revolver and, returning to the boulder, sat staring into the cold desert darkness for the remainder of that night.

Chapter Eight

Socorro
New Mexico Territory
September 1870

"May I help you folks with something?" asked Ike Wheeler, the owner of Socorro's only livery stable. Wheeler was a small, thin man who looked to be seventy years or so in age, but spry and stout enough to lug a bale of hay down from the loft or handle a mallet and anvil with no trouble at all.

"We're in need of a pony for the child here," Job said. Since they had discovered Missy Slatter abandoned and alone in the desert, she had ridden behind the mojo man on the albino mule. He figured it was high time they provided her with her own means of transportation.

The liveryman eyed the girl appraisingly and nodded. "I have a little red sorrel in the corral out back, and a saddle that should fit her well. Sixty dollars in all."

"Sounds agreeable to me. May I take a look at the critter?"

"Let me settle with this gentleman here and I'll show her to you." Wheeler turned and walked back to a man in black robes who was in the process of purchasing a gray donkey. When the agreed-upon amount had changed hands, the stable owner motioned to Job and they walked out back.

"Lookee here, Mister Eye!"

The gunfighter turned at Missy's voice. She was pointing at a weathered wanted poster tacked to one of the livery's double doors. He walked over and studied it.

WANTED
BAKER'S DOZEN
FOR BANK & STAGE ROBBERY
HORSE & CATTLE THIEVERY
& MURDER
REWARD: $5,000 DEAD OR ALIVE

Given what had happened to Missy's mother and sister, Dead-Eye figured torture and rape should have been added to the list of atrocities, but whoever had issued the notice and its bounty had been too tactful and polite to do so.

"They even put their pictures on there," said the little girl. As she studied the poster, she cuddled a doll Dead-Eye had bought her at the mercantile back in Tulerosa. The toy boasted a painted China face, curly yellow hair, and a blue gingham dress.

The Southerner nodded. The drawings were crude, but likely accurate enough to identify the thirteen men by sight. "A mangey-looking bunch, wouldn't you say?"

"I sure would," the girl said. A shade of fear and doubt lurked behind the anger in her blue eyes, "They appear to be hard men to be reckoned with. Mr. Eye, if you'd rather not..."

"That's already been settled on, Lil' Miss," Dead-Eye told her. He brought a shriveled finger to his blue lips. "And remember, it'd be best to keep our bargain betwixt ourselves. Ol' Job, he has a way of allowing common sense to step in and explain why something shouldn't be done as easily as why it ought to."

Missy made a gesture like buttoning her lips and gave the lanky dead man a wink. "He'll not hear a word from me."

They were examining a couple more posters nailed to the stable door— one for a fellow named John Wesley Hardin and another for a confidence man and gambler named Jefferson Randolph Smith the Second—when they were interrupted.

"Pardon me," came a gentle voice from behind them.

The two turned and regarded the one who had just bought the donkey. He was a man of average height with a swarthy complexion, clean-shaven face, and hair the darkness of pitch tar. He was dressed in the ankle-length cassock of a holy man, with a white collar around his throat and a golden crucifix hanging from a long rosery chain. He wore a flat-brimmed black hat with a rounded peak. From the left side of the hat's brim hung a single black tassel.

Dead-Eye nodded courteously. "What can we do for you, padre?"

"I was wondering if you might be traveling in the direction of Santa Fe?"

"We are, but we'll be turning westward and heading for Arizona territory before we get there," he answered. "Would you be wanting to travel with us?"

"Yes," said the man. He nodded toward the collection of posters on the barn door. "I put my trust in God with all earthly matters, but with hombres like those on the loose... well, it is always safer and more comforting to travel in the company of others, such as yourself."

Missy eyed him curiously. "Are you a preacher?"

He smiled. "In a manner of speaking. I am a priest of the Catholic faith. My name is Vasco Núñez."

"Your way of speaking is different from those south of the border," Dead-Eye observed. "You're not from Mexico or further down, are you?"

"I hail from Spain, across the sea. I am a servant of divinity from the Basilica of Santa Maria del Mar in the city of Barcelona."

"Is that a fancy name for a church house?" asked the child.

"Yes, it is a very large and beautiful cathedral. It is so massive that you would feel as though you were swallowed up by a great whale if you stood within its sanctuary."

"You mean, like Jonah and that big fish in the Bible?"

The holy man laughed warmly. "Most certainly... but without the misery poor Jonah endured for three agonizing days!"

A moment later, Job appeared around the corner leading a brownish-red pony with three white stockings and an equally pale streak that ran down its nose, from forehead to nostrils. "Look what I got here, little Miss Slatter."

The girl squealed and ran to the sorrel. "She's *beautiful!*" Missy giggled as the horse nuzzled her face, drawing in the scent of her.

"This here's my traveling partner, Job," Dead-Eye said in introduction. "Job, this here's Father Núñez from the country of Spain. He's asking to travel northward with us, if that's agreeable with you."

The two men regarded each other for a long moment before finally shaking hands. Dead-Eye detected a hint of hesitation and mutual distrust between the two men, which crossed him as puzzling, since he'd never seen the Louisiana mojo man react in such a way to a complete stranger. Usually, he was respectful and friendly.

"I suppose it wouldn't hurt none," Job finally said, his tone edged with caution. "Answer me one question, though, Father? Why have you left your home and traveled halfway around the world to this godforsaken place?"

"I have been sent here by the Church," the Spainard replied. "On a mission of great importance." But, beyond that, he did not elaborate.

Job examined him from head to toe. "Don't carry a gun, I see. In the territory we're riding through, that's not a point in your favor."

"I am sorry, but my sacred vows prevent me from possessing instruments of death and destruction."

"Considering the hellish things we've encountered during the past few years, I'd say it might be to our advantage having a holy man tagging along," Dead-Eye insisted, a bit peeved with how Job was reacting.

The negro shrugged his narrow shoulders. "If you care to vouch for him, I have no problem with him joining us. He just needs to keep our pace and pitch in with the chores along the way."

"Of course," promised Núñez. "However I may be of service, you may depend on me."

"I like him, Mister Job," Missy spoke up, hugging her new pony's neck. "Besides, having a preaching man along would be right comforting to me. You know, after having traveled with a couple of perfect heathens for so long and all." She suddenly thought better of her words and dropped her eyes. "I certainly meant no offense."

Job smiled at the girl and chuckled. "No offense taken, child. And for the record, we're far from perfect. All right then. If you want him to go, Missy, he's more than welcome."

After Ike Wheeler had finished saddling and tacking up the girl's pony, the four swung atop their mounts and left the town of Socorro, heading northward.

Dead-Eye and Job rode point, while the child and the Spanish priest trailed a few yards behind.

"A little rude to the padre back there, weren't you?" the dead man finally asked. "Did I detect a speck of jealousy on your part?"

"Are you kidding me?" replied Job with a roll of his eyes. "What the hell would I have to be jealous of?"

"I don't know. Maybe it's because you're both men of a spiritual nature. Perhaps you're vexed that he might know some things to combat Evangeline's evil that you don't have a clue about."

"I've told you time and time again... I ain't a particularly religious man. True, I use scripture and faith as tools and weapons at times, but only when deemed necessary."

A sly grin crossed Dead-Eye's pale face. "Hopefully you'll warm up to one another along the way. Maybe if you show him your Staff of Moses, he'll show you his Holy Grail or some such artifact."

"Well now you're just being downright blasphemous," Job snapped in disapproval.

"Yeah, I know," said the gunfighter, "being sort of half alive and half dead and all, I'm sort of stuck in limbo, betwixt Heaven and Hell."

"That's the God's honest truth, too. You could end up either strumming harp strings or shoveling coal," warned Job. "So, if I were you, I'd be damn careful who I was liable to piss off." The mojo man glanced over his shoulder. "Can't put my finger on it just yet, but there's just something about that feller that don't sit well with me."

Dead-Eye nodded and said nothing more concerning the subject. He'd kept company with Job long enough to know that the man had a keen sense for judging folks for what they were and weren't. If he had reservations about Vasco Núñez and his mysterious mission, then it certainly wasn't proper for him to balk or make light of it.

For several days they rode northward. To their east lay the winding channel of the Rio Grande, while to the west lay the barren desert that connected the New Mexico and Arizona territories. They came across no one during their journey and, truthfully, Dead-Eye and Job preferred it that way. It seemed that each new encounter was a potential courting with disaster, be it with mortal man or some being from the unknown.

They kept their wariness and suspicions to themselves, not wishing to alarm Missy Slatter. Considering that she had lost her immediate family in such a senseless and brutal manner, she remained sassy and spirited, anticipating the day when she laid eyes upon grandparents she had never met during her six years of life. Job fretted about her lack of sadness and grief, believing it wasn't natural for a small child to act otherwise, given the circumstances. Only Dead-Eye knew the pain and anger she held bottled up inside. And, because of his promise to the girl concerning the fate of Baker's Dozen, he felt it was a matter that only the two of them should share.

Another one that the mojo man worried over was the Spanish priest in the long black cassock. Vasco Núñez silently kept to himself at the rear of the procession and was polite and humble at the campfire at night, but remained stubbornly vague on the details of the mission the Catholic Church had sent him nearly six thousand miles across the world to accomplish.

On the fourth day of their sojourn through the blistering desert, Dead-Eye and Job reined their mounts abruptly to a halt and motioned for Missy and Núñez to do the same.

"Do you smell that?" asked the negro in the derby hat.

"I do," replied the zombie. "The odor of decay and rot... of raw meat and spilled blood... like the dregs of a slaughterhouse left in the hot sun to ripen and reek."

"What's that yonder?" piped the girl behind them. "Sparkling and turning round and round?"

They looked ahead and saw what the youngster was referring to. A small oval of darkness surrounded by spitting blue fire revolved in mid-air, lengthening and widening into a much larger opening. The bigger it grew, the stronger the stench of death and decay became. As the bottom of the portal touched the ground, something huge and hideous shambled from the shadows within with wet, sucking sounds.

"Looks like another confounded visitor from the Hole Out of Nowhere," said Dead-Eye. He swept back the side of his coat, revealing the sawed-off scattergun underneath, and drew the big, nickel-plated Dragoon pistol from its holster. "Coming to claim its pound of flesh, I'd wager."

Job's eyes widened as the creature departed its realm and invaded theirs. "Looks like you could be right on the nose with that assumption."

The being who squeezed through the otherworldly portal was not only huge, but obscenely massive in height and girth. If the two could have hazarded a guess, they would have determined it as measuring twelve feet from sky to earth and fifteen or so from one side to the other. It looked to be a glistening, crimson conglomeration of raw flesh and body parts. Some of its multitude of members and features were human in nature, but many had been appropriated from a variety of mammals, birds, and sea creatures. Even more of its horrid hodge-podge consisted of beings they had never laid eyes upon. Arms, legs, tentacles, every form and shape of appendage imaginable, flexed and flailed from its churning mass. A thousand eyes—mortal, animal, insectile, alien—regarded them with a yearning born of an insatiable appetite, while a hundred mouths, all gnashing teeth and fangs, spoke in a single thunderous voice.

"COME FORTH, SO I MAY TAKE POSSESSION OF YOU!" it demanded. As it shambled slowly toward them, the odor of torn and reassembled flesh and bone grew more pungent and offensive. Many of the limbs were bloated, festering with infection and gangrene.

Job grimaced at the awful stench of decomposition that filled the air. He glanced over his shoulder at the traveling priest. "You stay here with the child, Father. We'll ride out and converse with this monstrosity. If our meeting should go sour, take young Missy and flee to the nearest town you can find."

Vasco Núñez neither agreed nor disagreed. He sat atop his burrow and stared past Job and Dead-Eye, as though studying the abhorrent creature. But, for the time being, he stayed put and did not move.

Together, the two rode forward, slowly closing the distance between themselves and the grisly fiend.

"Have you got any idea of how to defeat this thing?" Dead-Eye asked his companion in a low tone. "I don't think bullets or buckshot are gonna do a damn bit of good. There's too much of it to inflict damage upon."

Job shook his head. "I believe you're right. And I don't think silver will slay it, either, like others we've fought. It's not supernatural in nature, as far as I can tell. It seems to be some sort of creature that absorbs its victims, alive and kicking, and makes them a part of it."

"You could use the Staff and bring locusts upon it, like you did that monstrous gar back at Horseshoe Bay in Louisiana."

"Perhaps," mused the mojo man, "but for now, let's see precisely what we're dealing with here."

They continued onward, then stopped when there was sixty feet between them and the putrescent being. The thing's multitude of eyes settled on the two, appraising them and what they had to offer.

"I'm guessing that the witch Evangeline sent you to deal with us, is that correct?" asked Job.

"WHAT YOU SURMISE IS TRUE," roared the abomination of conjoined viscera. "I AM DOLTHEMAR, THE COLLECTOR, AND THE DARK ENCHANTRESS HAS SENT ME HERE TO DISPATCH THE TWO OF YOU. SHE AND HER COMPANIONS ARE WEARY OF YOUR PURSUIT AND DESIRE YOU DEAD." Dozens upon dozens of grinning mouths marred the creature's crimson flesh. "OR, EVEN BETTER, DAMNED TO LIVE ONWARD THROUGH ME AND SUFFER HIDEOUSLY AND WITHOUT CEASING."

"And what sort of bounty did she offer you for completing the task?" Dead-Eye asked him out of curiosity.

"FOR A START, BOTH OF YOU TO ADD TO MY MENAGERIE OF FLESH," Dolthemar told him. "AFTER THAT, THE FREEDOM TO ROAM YOUR REALM WITHOUT HINDRANCE AND CONTRIBUTE TO MY ESSENCE, ONE UNFORTUNATE SOUL AT A TIME." A moist, bubbling chuckle rattled through a hundred hidden throats. "MY MASS—MY SHEER VASTNESS—SHALL KNOW NO BOUNDARY WHEN I FINALLY CHOOSE TO DEPART THIS PLACE."

Job looked over at the gunfighter. "Not quite an outcome I cotton to, do you?"

"Hell no. Now's the time to come up with some hellacious conjuring or such. Grab ahold of one of those voodoo charms around your neck and let's get this done, then we'll be on our way."

The mojo man frowned. "Fact of the matter is," he said in scarcely a whisper. "I'm still figuring the proper way of approaching this threat."

"Well, you'd best deliver a solution quickly or we're liable to be swallowed whole and become a part of this vile son of a bitch's entourage!"

"Pardon me," came a voice from behind them. "May I be of service?"

Job looked around, annoyed. Father Núñez sat on the gray donkey a few feet to their rear. "I thought I instructed you to stay with the girl."

The priest ignored his statement and swung down to the rocky earth. "I believe I can offer some assistance with this matter. Perhaps serve as a mediator between you gentlemen and this being."

"Oh, you do, do you?" The negro's voice was thick with sarcasm.

Dead-Eye studied the holy man. "Maybe the padre has had dealings with such things before," he suggested, a little peeved at the way Job was acting. "Maybe he knows the best way to handle this."

Job shrugged his narrow shoulders. "Well, by all means... be our guest. But don't go screaming to us when that thing grabs hold of you and drags you back into the dark world it came from."

Núñez nodded respectfully, then began to walk directly toward the grotesque form of raw flesh, muscle, and bodily fragments.

Dead-Eye cocked his head and eyed the man next to him with displeasure. "What's gotten into you? Why are you so damn suspicious of this feller?"

"I don't know," admitted Job. "Like I said before, there's something wrong about him that I can't rightly comprehend. Got a feeling in my gut."

The two watched as the priest closed the gap between himself and the being called Dolthemar. Soon, he was standing no more than eight feet away from the thing. They half expected one of the suckered tentacles to curl out and snatch him, but it didn't. The creature's collection of mismatched eyes centered on Núñez as he softly began to speak. The distance was too great for them to discern precisely what the priest said, but it was clear that there was no tremble or waver of anxiety or terror in his voice.

For a minute or two, a brief conversation between man and beast took place. Then Núñez nodded quietly in agreement, took a knife with a long, thin blade from the folds of his black robes, and walking to a boulder a few feet away, laid his hand upon the flat of the stone.

Job leaned forward in his saddle, his eyes squinting against the afternoon haze. "Just what the hell is he up to?"

Both were beyond surprised when the priest laid the blade against the bottom knuckle of his forefinger and, without pause, cleaved the digit from his hand.

"Shitfire!" rasped Dead-Eye. "What'd he go and do that for?"

They watched as the severed finger dropped into the dust. Vasco Núñez calmly took a white handkerchief from a side pocket and wrapped his mutilated hand, to help stem the flow of blood. Then he bent down, picked up the finger, and walked over to Dolthemar. The array of stolen mouths that decorated the monster's form smiled broadly with anticipation as the

Spaniard turned the stump of the finger and anchored it into the pulsating wall of raw flesh.

A low moan rolled through the desert air, part pleasure, part victory. Dolthemar's massive form shuddered, large nodules like goosebumps prickling the crimson tissue. Dead-Eye and Job watched in a mixture of fascination and revulsion as Núñez's lost finger twitched and flexed, nerves melding with nerves, surrendering to the creature's command.

Man and monstrosity said nothing more to one another. The otherworldly creature known as Dolthemar retreated into the sparkling hole of the portal and, with a loud *crack*, was gone.

Cradling his injured hand, Vasco Núñez walked back to his traveling companions.

"What was that all that about?" Dead-Eye asked him.

"I struck a bargain with Dolthemar," Núñez explained, "and you were granted a reprieve. It is only temporary, however. It shall return for you sometime in the future. I advise that you be prepared for that day."

Rather than gratitude, Job replied with an edge of mistrust in his voice. "Now, why would you be willing to give up a part of yourself to save us?"

The priest's face was grave, showing no pain or regret at the sacrifice he had made moments before. "It is crucial that I accomplish the mission that the Church has entrusted in me. The chance of my success lessens if you both are dead. A single finger is a small price to pay to honor the expectations of my superiors."

As Núñez took the reins of his donkey and joined the wide-eyed Missy Slatter, Dead-Eye regarded the mojo man. "Well, did that cure your suspicions about the good father?"

Job's expression was as cynical as ever. "No, to tell the truth, it enforced them even more."

Dead-Eye considered what he had witnessed and nodded. "I'm beginning to agree. What sort of holy man would offer himself as sacrament to something so vile and profane?"

Chapter Nine

Ancient Puebloan Ruins
New Mexico Territory
September 1870

Two days passed. The flatlands gradually gave way to a broad valley of towering buttes and lengthy ridges of fiery red stone. As they rode among the monoliths, they found traces of an ancient civilization. At first, only small things: a fragment of painted pottery or a random arrowhead. Then, as the evening sun began to set, they found themselves approaching the ruins of a long-abandoned village. Walls of stacked stone chinked with mud stood alone in places, while several buildings, a wall or two shy of being whole structures, were located here and there. As they rode through the ruins, they passed a large, sunken circular area bordered by walls and accessed by short stairways on all four sides.

"What would this be?" asked Missy with curiosity.

"It's a kiva," Job explained. "A place of ceremony. The Pueblo and Hopi tribes use them for spiritual rites and rituals. Matter of fact, I'd say this is the remainder of an old Puebloan village we're riding through right now."

"Given that it's only a couple hours till dusk, I figure we should bed down here for the night," Dead-Eye suggested. "That is, if no one's afeared of haints and such."

"Not me!" declared the girl atop her sorrel. "If they come trifling with me, I'll kick their ghostly rumps back to the grave!"

"If you intend to talk them away, I'd say you're the one to do it," agreed the gunfighter with a wry wink. "Sometimes you make me want to dig a ditch and pull the earth over my worm-eaten carcass, just to escape that sassy temperament of yours!"

"Aw, you're just funning me, Mister Eye! You'd be the last one I'd give a tongue-lashing to!"

As Dead-Eye and Missy bantered back and forth, Job eyed the Catholic priest at the rear of the procession. Núñez studied the kiva and the ruins around it with noticeable interest. Almost with a sense of dawning recognition, it seemed.

Could this place have some bearing on the mission he was sent to accomplish? the mojo man wondered to himself.

They found a tall structure with three sturdy walls left standing and made their camp within its shelter for the night. Dead-Eye and Father Núñez gathered mesquite wood and dry brush for a fire, while Job unpacked a couple of iron pans and cooking utensils from one of Balaam's canvas packs. The tall Southerner spotted a long-eared jackrabbit on the run and dispatched it with a single shot to contribute to the vittles. As darkness fell, Job conjured a stew of rabbit meat, wild onions, creole spices, and a potato he'd purchased back in Socorro for just such an occasion. He mixed cornmeal and canteen water into a batter, then covering the second skillet with a lid, baked a generous pan of cornbread.

Sitting around the campfire, they leisurely feasted on the vittles that the Louisiana man had prepared, except for Dead-Eye, who witnessed their hunger stoically, his stomach no longer capable of accepting food and his bowels having lost the ability to the digest it.

Midway through the meal, Vasco Núñez looked across the flames of the fire and found Job staring at him. "During our travels, I have sensed that you do not take kindly to my presence," he said without hesitation.

The negro sipped coffee from a tin cup and shrugged his narrow shoulders. "Can't say I harbor any real animosity for you, padre. It just seems odd that we've traveled with you for nearly a week now and you've not bothered to let us in on what this urgent mission is that you've traveled halfway around the world to accomplish." Job eyed the Spaniard's bandaged hand. "And, I must admit, I'm a mite disturbed concerning what happened back yonder with the ogre Dolthemar. Never known a man of God to give himself—or any part, body or soul—to something so monstrous and unholy."

The priest seemed unphased by the mojo man's scathing words. "I have no reservations about revealing my mission to you. If you are so anxious to know, I will be happy to tell you. As for my bargain with Dolthemar, I did it purely for the benefit of you, the gunfighter, and young Missy. I have an extensive knowledge of such beings and their ways, and have sanctified cursed lands and their inhabitants before, as well as performed exorcisms in the name of the Church. Since you seemed at a loss of how to approach or conquer the fiend, I took it upon myself to stave off his ravenous advance."

"And we're obliged to you for it," said Dead-Eye. Job glowered at his traveling partner for his statement, but the zombie paid him no mind.

"You are welcome," replied Núñez with a graceful nod. "Now... about my mission. Before I tell you, I must impart to you a tale concerning my people, as well as those who once inhabited this territory now known as New Mexico. In fact, they may have even lived among the very ruins we now congregate in."

Job set his coffee aside and, reaching into a vest pocket, withdrew his pipe. He tamped a charge of tobacco into the bowl and lit it with a sulfur match. "Go ahead... we're listening."

Vasco Núñez leaned forward from where he sat. The flickering glow of the campfire danced across the forehead and cheekbones of his face. "In the year of our Lord 1540, under the supreme command of King Phillip the Second, a Spanish explorer by the name of Juan de Oñate Salazar moved northward from Peru and Mexico to the territory now known as Santa Fe. Accompanying him were two military commanders—Gaspar Espejo and Salazar's nephew Juan de Zaldívar—an order of six Catholic priests, and an army of two hundred men."

Missy Slatter idlily ran her fingers through her dolly's hair, making it curlier than it was before. "Conquistadors."

The three men looked at her. "Now, how in Sam Hill do you know that, Lil Miss?" asked Dead-Eye.

"My ma was a schoolmarm before she wed my pa," the girl said proudly. "I know all kinds of things."

The priest frowned at the word and its distasteful meaning. "Conquerors in your eyes perhaps, but in Spain they are regarded as explorers and heroes of the commonwealth." Núñez seemed slightly annoyed at the interruption. "So, on to my story. By the king's command, they were to govern the inhabitants of this land and convert them to the Catholic faith. The native people—Ácoma Pueblo—resisted Salazar's command, turning the Spaniards' lives into a living purgatory. Decades of conflict culminated in a grave dispute that led to the murderous ambush of thirteen Spaniards, including their commander Zaldivar, at the murderous hands of the savages. In turn, Salazar retaliated with his forces and, by the end of the battle, eight hundred to a thousand Ácoma were killed."

"Would that be warriors only?" asked Dead-Eye. "Or women and children as well?"

"Many fell that day, both young and old, man and woman," the priest said dryly. "Sometimes to right a great wrong, those who oppose you must be eliminated. But as fate would have it, a band of forty Ácoma braves, led by a Puebloan shaman called Kajika, overcame Gaspar Espejo and two dozen soldiers somewhere in the desert south of Santa Fe. Espejo and his men were cruelly tortured and mutilated, then tightly wrapped in strips of leather and staked to the earth in the hot noonday sun. The heat shrank the leather they were bound in, constricting and crushing the very life from them. It was then said that Kajika and his followers concealed their remains in some unknown location, where Salazar would never find them."

When they sensed that Vasco Núñez was at the end of his tale, Job drew smoke from his pipe and eyed the priest from across the fire. "A tale of evil men who outstepped their boundaries and paid for their indiscretions in spades, that's to be sure," he said. "But what does it have to do with your mission in coming to America?"

"In Spain, these men are still considered to be heroes of our nation," the priest told him. "Martyrs! Therefore, the archbishop of the Basilica, by order of the royal hierarchy, has bestowed upon me the task of locating the remains of Espejo and his soldiers and administering the last rites. For the wrongful humiliation they suffered, they are deserving of that courtesy."

"I reckon that's a matter of opinion," said Dead-Eye. "I'd say the thousand Ácoma who were slaughtered might feel differently."

"Do you know where their remains might be concealed?" Job asked. "We're intending to head westward tomorrow at sunrise, so you'll be on your own after that."

"I was made privy to pages from a journal written by a member of Espejo's militia who escaped their terrible fate," Núñez told him. "It gives vague directions to the area where the bodies of the commander and his soldiers might possibly be found. It may take some doing, but I shall succeed."

Missy Slatter studied the priest from where she sat at Dead-Eye's feet. "If those men did the evil things you claim they did, wouldn't they already be burning in Hell? What good is praying over their bones gonna do now?"

The priest smiled gently at the child. "What does a sweet and innocent child such as yourself know about Heaven and Hell?"

A grin crossed the gunfighter's gaunt face. "Don't let her appearance fool you, padre. She's not as sweet or innocent as you believe. If anyone knows Paradise and Purgatory, and who belongs there or not, it's Lil' Miss here."

The girl looked up from her doll. The grim expression in her blue eyes was more jaded and much older than what a girl her age should possess. "I think I'll visit with Pa for a while." Then she left the campfire and walked to where the animals and their cargo rested for the night.

"I didn't intend to upset the child," Vasco said, watching her go. "It may not be my place to say so, but she should allow her father to be buried, so she can grieve in a proper manner."

Job shook his head. "I've suggested that at every town we've ridden through, but she's as stubborn as a tick on a hound's ass. She's bound and determined that her pa is gonna be laid to earth in the family plot in Arizona."

"Given all that the poor young'un's been through," said Dead-Eye, "I'd say she's rightfully deserving of that consideration."

Around three o'clock the following morning, Dead-Eye felt a firm hand grasp his shoulder and shake him violently awake.

His gun hand acted before he could even open his eyes. The big Colt Dragoon was drawn, cocked, and shoved forcefully beneath the offender's nose, quicker than a heartbeat.

When the gunfighter studied the man's face in the glow of his foxfire-infected eye, he discovered it was Job.

"I don't need a third nostril," said the negro, taking hold of the pistol's barrel and slowly lowering it from his face. "I got two that work well enough already."

"You should know not to take me by surprise like that!" Dead-Eye grumbled, sitting up from where he lay.

"And your zombified state shouldn't allow you the luxury of sleep, neither. You ought to be wide awake and on guard all hours of the night. You've been slipping lately. Looks like I might need to cast a spell of insomnia upon you... as well as something to quell those confounded nightmares you suffer nightly."

The dead man rose to his feet. "What was so danged important that you had to rattle my bones that way?"

"Father Núñez is gone. I got up to take a piss and he was nowhere to be found. His burrow and gear are still here, but he's vanished." The mojo man eyed the carpetbag lashed to the donkey's saddle. "And since he's absent, I have a mind to do a little snooping."

Together, they walked across the campsite to where the priest's animal was tethered next to a fragment of ancient wall. Dead-Eye shook his head in disapproval as Job opened the flap of the satchel and rummaged through its contents. "It's disrespectful, pilfering through a holy man's private belongings. The Lord has struck folks down stone-cold dead for much less."

"I told you before," said the black man, whispering so as not to awaken Missy Slatter several yards away, "there's something that's not altogether right about that man." Finally, he located something of interest. He withdrew a long white envelope with a seal of red wax on the back flap. Job opened the envelope and, withdrawing a letter, unfolded it. When he couldn't make out the handwriting in the gloom, he reached up, grabbed the bristles of Dead-Eye's mustache, and yanked his head down closer to the paper. The Southerner's left eye illuminated the page with a pale glow. "Sorry, but I was in need of some reading light."

"What does it say?"

Job grinned, his suspicions vindicated. "Just as I thought! He's been excommunicated!"

"Defrocked? For what reason?"

"This missive is directly from the Vatican," Job explained. "It says that he has been cast out for indulging in dark rituals, witchcraft, and keeping company with demons and such!"

"So, that's how come he was so chummy with Ol' Dolthemar," said Dead-Eye. "Where do you suppose he's gone now?"

Job looked off into the darkness beyond the crumbling walls of the Puebloan ruins. "I'd say this is the place he came to find. That story he told at the campfire was probably factual… but I bet his true mission isn't the one he led us to believe."

"Probably out in those ruins right now," said Dead-Eye with a scowl. "Up to no good."

"I'd say just let him get on with his business… but if it's unholy business, I'm not one to stand for such. You should know that by now."

The gunfighter's countenance grew solemn. "Me neither."

"Go yonder and check on the girl before we head out looking for him," Job suggested.

Dead-Eye nodded and did as he asked. A moment later, he stared down at the child bundled up a woolen blanket, only her hair showing from beneath the folds of the cloth. Something about the way she laid didn't set well with the man, so he pulled the edge of the cover back, just to make sure.

"Well, I'll be damned!"

"What's wrong?" asked Job, joining him.

"It's that yeller-haired doll!" he said, pointing at the toy that had taken the youngster's place. "Lil' Miss is gone, too."

"Knowing her curious disposition, could be that she saw Núñez leave and snuck off after him."

Dead-Eye's hand dropped to the butt of his forty-four. "Or he might have taken her… to make use of in some devilish way."

The two wasted no time. They quickly went to their mounts and saddled them, then swung atop the black Morgan and white mule. Soon, they were heading into the pitch darkness of early morning, their hearts heavy with dread… afraid for the well-being of the orphaned child who had been entrusted into their care.

Chapter Ten

In the Underground Catacombs
New Mexico Territory
September 1870

Missy Slatter crouched behind a clump of prickly pear cactus, careful not to poke herself with the plant's sharp quills. She watched as a dark form circled the border of the kiva, holding the lit stub of a candle ahead of him.

Vasco Núñez had given Dead-Eye the slip, but not her. She had watched from the folds of her blanket as he had risen from his bedroll, taken a few objects from his carpet bag, and then vanished into the night. Curious, she had left a decoy in her place and followed him at a distance. She didn't rightly know what he was up to, but she figured it had something to do with that tale of conquistadors and Indian warriors he had shared at the campfire only a few hours before.

After walking the upper level of the ceremonial area twice, the priest made his way down the stone steps to the basin of the kiva. As swift as a fox, Missy left the concealment of the cactus and made it to a cluster of boulders unseen. Closer than she had been before, she watched the man in the black cassock with interest. Núñez stood in the very center of the kiva, his head bowed. Whether the gesture was due to prayer or deep thought, Missy couldn't say. Then he lifted his head and his face was revealed by the glow of the candle. He scowled frightfully and, breaking the chain of the rosary around his neck, flung the golden crucifix away in disgust.

Then he walked to a dark entranceway in one of the inner walls of the kiva and was swallowed up by the shadows within.

Again, Missy crept forward, anxious to follow Núñez and witness the ritual he had traveled so far to execute. She had never seen someone administer last rites before. *Well, I'm sure gonna lay eyes on it now,* she told herself. Taking care, she scrambled down the staircase, crossed the circular space of the kiva, and ducked through the dark doorway that the Spaniard had entered.

At first the blackness beyond the portal was dense and disorienting. Then she detected the faint glow of the priest's candle. But the light didn't shine from ahead, but rather from *below*. She tested the stone floor ahead of her and discovered that a steep set of steps descended downward. Cautiously, she took one sandstone riser at a time and made her way down a narrow passageway that led to a dark hollow beneath the floor of the kiva. The air was dry and stank of dust and ancient timbers... as well as something else. Something old, decayed, and long forgotten.

When she reached the bottom, she found herself in a huge, barrel-shaped chamber. Apparently, Father Núñez had lit the dry tinder of a half-dozen torches along the circular wall with the flame of his single candle. She stood in the doorway for a long moment, looking for the man, but he was nowhere to be found.

She wandered into the hollow of the big room and crossed the ornate floor, which was decorated with painted symbols and drawings... as well as long-congealed puddles of blood. Lots of blood. Missy lifted her eyes and studied the chamber's construction. The flat of the kiva overhead was supported by great timbers that had been anchored into the stone floor, as well as a wagon wheel pattern of equally strong beams across the ceiling above her. In the center of the ceremonial chamber was a rectangular pedestal of heavy stone. It was streaked and stained with the sanguine ichor of some long-ago victim... or victims.

But it was the things that were bound to the walls of the underground sanctuary that thrilled her tiny heart and sent a chill through her youthful bones.

Lashed to the stones by thick strands of braided rawhide were the remains of a couple dozen men. They were wrapped tightly with thin strips of dry, cracked leather and all that shown from their bindings were their skeletal hands and the stark and eyeless bone of their fleshless skulls. Their jaws gaped, unhinged and open, as though they had perished in intense agony and terror.

Missy remembered something she had seen back in El Paso when she was a year younger. A traveling sideshow had come to town and, along with acrobatic dwarfs, a man as strong as Hercules, and a woman with pictures on her skin from head to toe, was another attraction. In a strange casket—a sarcophagus the man at the ticket booth had called it—was the bony remains of a man wrapped in dusty cloth bandages. She recalled her mother telling her that the thing had come from the pyramids of Egypt and that it was the mummy of an ancient pharaoh. Looking at the collection of corpses that hung on the circular wall of the underground chamber, Missy knew that these things were mummies, too. Ones that had been tortured and slain in the blistering New Mexico sun, before being hauled deep into the pit and hidden there, where Juan de Oñate Salazar and his remaining conquerors could never find them.

"It pains me to see them this way," said a voice behind her. "Treated with disgrace and utter disregard. Such brave and stalwart souls, tormented and murdered by the blood-drenched hands of heartless barbarians."

Startled, Missy whirled. Vasco Núñez stood only a few feet away. His bronze face was impassive, but a wild fire burned deep within his dark eyes. She was surprised to see that his clothing was not the simple, ankle-length cassock that he had worn since they had first met him in the town of Socorro, but a thick black robe with a hood that covered his head and nearly concealed his features in shadow. Around his shoulders hung vestments of deep violet and crimson, patterned like the descending body and triangular head of some horrid serpent. Dangling from his throat, in place of the crucifix, was an iron pentagram with the wicked head of a horned goat set in the center.

"That one," he told her, pointing at one of the skeletal forms. "That is the remains of Gaspar Espejo. He led his valiant soldiers to the very end... as he shall once again... and very soon." Núñez studied the child and smiled. His teeth seemed long and predatory. "I considered abducting you and bringing you here against your will, but I knew your meddling curiosity would get the better of you. You did not disappoint me."

Missy glanced toward the dark doorway that led upward to the surface of the kiva. She took a few quick steps in that direction, but was swiftly intercepted by the man in black. He grabbed her by the wrist with one strong hand, while drawing a long-bladed dagger from his sash with the other. He held the edge of the knife against the pale column of Missy's throat and, slowly, began to guide her toward the blood-stained altar.

"Are... are you going to do what you came here for?" she asked, frightened and confused. "The last rites?"

"No, mi niña," rasped the dark priest in her ear. "I have come here to resurrect those who were so wrongfully captured and slaughtered. And, unfortunately for you, that requires a sacrifice of blood!"

Dead-Eye and Job left Brimstone and Balaam where they stood and walked to the edge of the kiva. The gunfighter held the big Dragoon pistol in one hand and the sawed-down twelve-gauge in the other. Job toted the brass-framed Henry rifle. His pepperbox pistol protruded from his belt, ready to be drawn and fired.

"So, you think this is where they went?" asked the dead man. The luminance of his blind eye cast a pale glow over the ceremonial area below them. "I see nary a sign of them. Not even footprints."

"See that opening yonder?" The negro pointed to the dark entranceway in the wall of the lower level. "I'd say there is a chamber underneath this kiva where council was held... maybe even tribal rituals. It may be the place the padre was searching for."

They walked to the stone steps and were heading into the hollow of the ceremonial circle, when a shrill scream echoed from the direction of the shadowy passageway. They didn't need to hear it twice to know it came from Missy Slatter.

"Come on!" Dead-Eye led the way, his gaunt face grim and his bony hands filled with gunmetal. Job was close on his heels, the Henry levered and ready.

They entered the opening and made their way down the stone steps that led to the catacombs beneath the ceremonial kiva. Dead-Eye's foxfire eye cast a yellow glow upon the surrounding walls and the descending stairs, illuminating the way. A moment later, they stepped through a lower doorway and found themselves facing an unnerving tableau.

Missy was hogtied and laying atop the stone altar, writhing and thrashing. At the head of the sacrificial slab stood Vasco Núñez. The dark priest was decked out in ebony robes, his hands raised over head as he chanted an incantation in an unknown tongue. His face was rigid and gleamed with sweat, while his eyes were bright with an unholy fervor. One of his outstretched hands was empty, while the other held an ornate dagger with a wickedly long blade.

"Look!" said Job. "Along the walls!"

The mummified remains of Gaspar Espejo and his conquistadors hung motionlessly at first. Then, slowly, they began to jerk, their joints creaking and the bones trapped within the confinement of leather wrapping rattling with protest, aching to be free. Their neckbones popped and crackled as their heads rotated, regarding the young victim atop the altar with empty eye sockets. From the black pits, yellow scorpions swarmed. They dropped to the stone floor and skittered toward the gunfighter and the mojo man, their tails cocked and ready to strike.

At the same time, Dead-Eye saw that the girl had slowly ceased her fighting. She grew limp upon the altar. Her robust face turned as pale as lard and her blue eyes, customarily full of piss and vinegar, became glassy and unfocused. "What's he doing to Lil' Miss?" he asked in alarm.

"The bastard's siphoning away her life force!" Job told him. "Transferring it to those carcasses on the walls!" As they started forward, the negro noticed that Núñez had ceased his chanting. Both hands entwined tightly around the haft of the dagger now. "He's intent on completing the ritual with a blood sacrifice!"

"Rise my brethren!" commanded the wayward priest. "Rise and exact your vengeance!"

As Núñez brought the knife downward, intending to impale the child, Dead-Eye raised the Dragoon and snapped off a single shot. The bullet hit the flat of the blade just as it passed before the priest's feverish face. The slug sheared steel in half and drove the razor-sharp fragment backward, impaling the man's left eye. Núñez sank to his knees in agony, dropping the broken dagger and grasping at the metal that protruded from his skull. Optical fluid and blood gushed from the socket, bathing his face and hands. The gunfighter ended his torment a moment later, putting a second forty-four bullet through his right eye. The projectile burrowed through the orb of his eyeball, tunneled through the tender tissue of his brain beyond, and exited an instant later in an explosion of bone fragments and blood.

Job looked down and saw that the swarm of scorpions was nearly upon them. He grabbed the chicken foot that hung from the choker of charms around his neck and waved it up and down, to and fro, chanting a spell beneath his breath as he did so. Almost immediately, the creatures began to shrivel up and die. Before long, nothing was left of them but empty husks and dust.

Dead-Eye ran forward and drew the Bowie knife from the sheath beneath his coat. He quickly cut the bindings around Missy Slatter's wrist and feet and hefted her over his shoulder like a sack of potatoes. "What about these dried-up sons of bitches?" he asked as he backed away from the altar.

The rawhide that had held the desecrated remains of Espejo and his men for nearly two hundred and eighty years parted as they flexed and surged against their bonds. "There's no stopping them now," Job told him. "They won't become full-blown flesh-and-bone men like Núñez intended, but they have enough of Missy's stolen spirit in them to keep them reanimated and coming after us."

Two broke free of their imprisonment and shambled toward Dead-Eye and the child that lay limply across his shoulder. The tall Southerner holstered his revolver, then cocked the twin hammers of the sawed-down scattergun and fired from the hip. The blast of double-aught buckshot cut the pair in half. Even then, their upper halves convulsed and shuddered on the floor of the underground chamber, and slowly began to crawl toward them. Skeletal fingers grated coarsely against the painted stones, drawing them forward.

"Let's get the hell out of here!" Job lifted the repeating rifle to his shoulder and unleashed a volley of shots, working the lever as he squeezed the trigger. Holes opened in the bony foreheads of several mummies that had broken loose, but it seemed to have no effect on them. They continued onward, their skeletal arms outstretched, hungering for retribution.

They had been brought back from the dead for one purpose and one only—to destroy with unrestrained malice, completely devoid of conscience or mercy.

Chapter Eleven

The Kiva of the ancient Ácoma
New Mexico Territory
September 1870

A moment later, they were up the stone stairway and standing on the flat of the kiva's surface. Dawn had come while they had been underground and they squinted against the brilliance of sunrise as it peaked the eastern horizon. Behind them, they could hear the scurrying of the leatherbound mummies fighting their way through the narrow shaft of the staircase, naked bone rasping coarsely against time-smoothened stone.

"How many of those things are there?" Job asked, feeding more cartridges into the Henry's loading port.

"Besides the two I cut in half, I'd say nearly two dozen." Dead-Eye laid the child on the floor of the kiva. He was concerned with her sickly complexion and listlessness. She moaned softly and stared up at him. It was as though her gaze looked right through him. "What about silver? Will that stop the magic that's resurrected them?"

"That's what this here Henry was loaded with," the negro told him. "Shot a couple square in the brainpan and it didn't do a damned thing!"

Dead-Eye broke the shotgun open, extracted the spent shells from the breech, and replaced them with fresh ones. "You got some spell to cast upon them? Maybe the same one you used back in Oklahoma when those dead Cherokee braves sprouted out of the earth and came after us?"

"I solved that problem by laying flesh and sinew upon their bones.

We survived because, deep down, they were good men to begin with. I'm sure as hell not gonna restore an army of men who did their share of slaughtering and looting in their lifetimes. If Núñez had succeeded and sacrificed the girl like he intended, more than likely that's precisely what would have happened."

Dead-Eye let the twelve-gauge hang by its sling and began to thumb forty-four cartridges into the rechambered Dragoon. He looked up and saw Brimstone and Balaam standing on the lip of the kiva wall, staring down at them. "Take Lil' Miss and get her away from here. I have an idea of how to stop these fiends."

Job shouldered the repeating rifle by its sling and gathered the child in his arms. She hung limply in his grasp like someone at the point of death. Quickly, he mounted the stone steps and headed for the white mule. "I'll tend to Missy and see if I can bring her back to health," he called down to the gunfighter. "What do you have in mind?"

Dead-Eye raised his fingers to his blue lips and whistled shrilly. In response, Brimstone leapt down into the circle of the ceremonial kiva. The black Morgan trotted to his master, who stepped into a stirrup and swung onto the saddle. "I'm gonna finish the job the Ácoma started three centuries ago!"

Job slung Missy over his shoulder and climbed atop Balaam. With a crack of the reins, the mule took off in the direction of the place where they had camped the night before.

Suddenly, the dark entranceway from below was choked with the mummified remains of Gaspar Espejo's soldiers. At the same time, the baked clay of the kiva's floor began to crack open around the gunfighter and his horse. Skeletal hands burst through, clawing, hauling the bodies they were attached to into the open. Soon, the revived remains of Espejo and his men began to surge forward from all directions, eager to surround and overtake them.

Dead-Eye leaned down and whispered into the ear of the demonic steed. "You're a master of hellfire. Let's heat up this pit for these skinny-ass scoundrels!"

Brimstone's eyes flared from muted red to brilliant crimson. Lithe muscles flexed and rippled beneath the black hide of the horse as he leapt over several mummies into the outer area near the curved wall of the kiva. The Morgan began to gallop around the cluster of resurrected Spaniards in a broad circle, building speed with each fall of his hooves.

As the army of living dead twisted and turned, attempting to surge toward the horse and its rider, Dead-Eye drew his Dragoon revolver and took steady aim. With each shot, he shattered the kneecap of one of the advancing mummies. Three pitched forward and collapsed, no longer able to stand. The gunfighter lifted the barrel of his pistol skyward, ejected the spent brass, and quickly reloaded. Then he continued to drop the skeletal soldiers one by one.

As his master performed his task, so did Brimstone. The black horse lifted his head skyward and expelled bursts of fiery breath from his nostrils and mouth. Soon, the air above the pit swirled with a turbulent maelstrom of hellfire. The cloud of flame spun like the center of a cyclone, sending waves of unbearable heat downward toward the shambling occupants of the kiva. Dead-Eye ducked his head and clung tight to the reins. The metal of the big pistol grew red hot in his fist and his hat and clothing began to smolder with the fire that rained from above.

Gradually, the heat took a toll on the mummies as well. The leather strips that encased them began to constrict as the temperature of the air around them continued to rise. Dead-Eye heard their bones begin to pop and crack as their bindings shrank, hindering their movements and stopping them in their tracks.

The tall Southerner and his horse leapt from the shallow pit, landing on the earth that surrounded the kiva. They watched grimly as the heat of Brimstone's infernal breath reached its pinnacle. The strips of rawhide that entwined the living carcasses of Espejo and his men grew so hard and rigid that their remaining bones abruptly crumbled and turned to dust.

A moment later, the swirling cloud of hellfire dissipated and was gone. All that remained on the floor of the kiva was a scattering of scorched leather swathing and gritty gray powder.

Before long, Dead-Eye had returned to the ruins where they had made camp the night before. He was relieved to find Missy Slatter sitting up, carefully taking water from a canteen. The color was returning to her freckled cheeks and her eyes were weary but possessed the same youthful spark as before.

"What did you do to break the padre's spell?" he asked his traveling partner.

"I didn't," said Job. "You did. The moment you conquered those confounded things, her health was returned to her."

Dead-Eye crouched and placed a hand on the child's shoulder. "How are you fairing, Lil' Miss?"

"Weaker than watered-down whiskey," she told him, "but I'm feeling a mite better."

"Why do you reckon Núñez traveled halfway around the world to resurrect those dead conquistadors?" the gunfighter asked Job. "What was his purpose in doing so?"

The little mojo man shrugged his shoulders. "Beats me. Revenge more than likely. Either for his nation or his own satisfaction. Could be he was kin to one of the Spaniards that Kajika and his braves brought justice to, or perhaps he was a descendant of Gaspar Espejo himself. Whatever his intentions, he'll rot in the hole where his countrymen were confined for nearly three hundred years."

Dead-Eye nodded. "I'd say he'll make a favorable home for scorpions, spiders, and such, that's for sure."

"Let's allow the girl to regain her bearings, then head west for Arizona territory. It's barely past daybreak and I'm ready to get clear of this confounded place."

"I'll lash the supplies to Balaam and Missy's pa to Brimstone," replied the cadaverous gunman, turning to leave.

"Could you grab my dolly before you go?" asked the girl.

Dead-Eye walked over, lifted the yellow-haired doll from the tangle of blankets, and brought it to her. "Here... but don't use it to pull the wool over our eyes again. If you do, I'll feed her to Brimstone. Believe me, he'll eat her, China head and all."

The girl wrinkled her nose in distaste. "You smell like you've been roasted in a smokehouse, Mister Eye. And your suit is all scorched and sooty."

The tall man grinned. "When Ol' Brimstone lets the Hell inside him loose, there's no dodging it. Besides, I might find a tailor and purchase a new set of duds when we get you to Holbrook. These are growing downright threadbare and a mite gamey."

"I'd say you're the one who's gamey," Job said. "From the inside out."

Dead-Eye cast a baleful eye at his traveling partner. "You sure as hell don't smell like a saloon girl's bubble bath yourself. Although, in your case, it wouldn't be a bad idea to seek one out once we reach town."

"Hush! It's not proper to speak of such in front of the child!"

"Aw, I know all about whores," said Missy, fiddling with her doll's golden hair. "Ma called 'em soiled doves. They always looked right clean to me, all painted up and pretty like."

Dead-Eye chuckled at the disturbed look on the negro's face. "Don't you recollect? This little gal knows all kinds of things... and she's got a soft spot in her heart for whores and such. I bet she's got a special place for sawed-off little witch doctors, too." Then, he headed to where the animals were tethered, eager to ready them for the journey ahead.

Chapter Twelve

The Painted Desert
Arizona Territory
Early October 1870

"Is it them?"

Job lay on his belly on the lip of a rocky ledge. He peered through the eyepiece of his spyglass, studying the vast expanse of the Arizona desert that stretched beneath them. Dead-Eye and Missy Slatter crouched next to him, anxious to learn what the telescope revealed.

"There's thirteen of them," said the mojo man. "They have twenty-two horses with them. The ones they're riding, along with nine others... stolen, more than likely." He focused on the rider in the lead. "One is missing his left arm. Seems like you mentioned such a fella before, didn't you, child?"

Missy nodded. "It was Otis Baker himself. He was crippled on one side, but could draw and shoot a gun well enough with the other."

Dead-Eye surveyed the sky with his one good eye. The sunset of crimson, violet, and gold was beginning to deepen as evening began to give way to nightfall.

"Are they riding onward? The hour is growing late, but then outlaws are known to travel at night when they're on the lam."

Job studied the layered mounds of the badlands below. "Looks like they're making camp in a hollow between two hills, so I reckon they'll be there till sunrise." He crept back a yard or so, then stood and folded the spyglass, returning it to a leather pouch on his belt. "If that's Baker's

Dozen down there, my advice is to head eastward and put as many miles between us and them as possible. When we come to a town or military fort, we can tell 'em what we saw, and they can deal with the scalawags the way they see fit."

"You mean, ride east tonight?" asked the six-year-old with concern. "Without a bite of supper or a good night's sleep?"

"That would be the safest thing to do. You remember what they did to your folks. If we chance staying here, we might end up the same way."

The three turned and walked to where they had begun to set up their own camp. Luckily, the wood and brush of their fire had not yet been lit. If it had been, the desperados would have probably seen and smelled the smoke, then come looking for the source.

Before they got there, Dead-Eye broke away from the other two, heading in a different direction. Missy seemed alarmed as the tall Southerner leisurely made his way to his horse.

"Maybe you shouldn't, Mister Eye," she called out to him.

Job paused and looked toward the gunfighter, his eyes narrowing. "Shouldn't *what*?" He watched as the dead man drew his revolver from its holster and checked its loads, then did the same with the shotgun beneath his coat. "What in tarnation are you up to?"

"I made a promise to Lil' Miss there," Dead-Eye told him. "And I aim to keep it."

Missy took a few hesitant steps toward him. "I ain't gonna fault you if you'd prefer not to. It's too dangerous. I hate an Indian giver more than anything, but I'll make an exception in your case."

Dead-Eye turned toward the girl, his face rigid with cold determination. "No, ma'am. I'll not go back on my word."

"So, what is it you're intending to do?" asked Job. "What have you two been plotting behind my back?"

"I'm going down to smite the infidels on behalf of young Missy," he replied. "For the pain and misery they put her and her kin through. We made a pact a while ago. I aim to keep my end of the bargain."

"So, you're just gonna ride down there and take on the whole bunch of 'em? You, your pistol, and your scattergun against thirteen bloodthirsty murderers armed to the teeth? That's downright suicide!"

Dead-Eye grinned. "A man can't kill himself, or be killed, if he's already dead. That's to my advantage."

"They'll shoot you to pieces, Mister Eye!" wailed the little girl. "Let's do as Mister Job suggested and ride east."

But the gunfighter's objective couldn't be swayed. "I shall go down there and rain retribution upon those sorry sons of bitches," he told her. "Besides, old sawbones Frankenstein there will plug me up and put me back together, like he's done a dozen times before."

Job looked doubtful. "There's only so much damage I can fix. You come back in the worse way, and there might not be anything I can do for you."

"I'll take that chance."

"Are you aiming to confront them tonight? After they fall asleep?"

Dead-Eye swung atop Brimstone and turned toward a narrow trail that descended toward the floor of the desert. "No. I'll allow them their rest and kill them bright and early in the morning. They'll be sore and slow from sleeping on the hard ground all night. Their reflexes will be hindered. That'll prove to be in my favor."

"An aching back and a stiff neck won't hinder their trigger fingers none," warned the mojo man. "Are you planning to ride in, guns blazing, and take them by surprise?"

"I haven't decided yet," said the tall Southerner as he rode away. "I'll figure that out on the way down."

The little black man seemed torn with indecision. "You want I should go with you?"

"No, you stay here with Lil' Miss. This is my promise to keep, not yours. You might loan me that pepperbox of yours, though, in case I should have need of it."

Job took the little .36-caliber pistol from a vest pocket and handed it to him. "You're the stubbornest polecat of a man I ever did know!" he said with a scowl. Then his eyes softened. "You know your son is depending on you to save him from the clutches of Jules Holland and his unholy quartet. If you go getting blown to smithereens, it ain't gonna do him—or us—a bit of good."

"I'll be back. You've got my word on it." Then he snapped the reins and spurred the black horse forward.

"Take care, Mister Eye!" Missy called after him.

Dead-Eye turned and gave the little girl a nod and a wink. Then he studied Job's dark face once again. The expression in the negro's eyes was none too pleased, although he could detect a definite trace of concern as well.

As Brimstone cautiously made his way down the narrow trail toward the basin of the Painted Desert, Dead-Eye leaned down and spoke in the horse's ear. "When the lead starts flying, stay put and leave it to me. Those bastards are mine."

The black Morgan snorted and, unseen by his master, rolled his eyes. Like Job, he didn't cotton much to the deadly bargain Dead-Eye had made with the tow-headed Texas girl... or what was liable to happen to him during the undertaking of such.

The first rays of dawn pressed against Otis Baker's eyelids, rousing him from his sleep. He stretched, yawned, and farted, then rocked forward out of his blankets. It took several tries. After a rebel cannonball had sheared off his left arm at Spotsylvania in '64, Otis had discovered it to be difficult to rise from a lying or sitting position, or to even mount a horse. But, being the kind of man he was, he was too proud to ask for assistance. Usually, he strained and huffed for a minute or two as he fought to gain his balance and stand to his feet. No one laughed at his disability, though. His men respected him too much to do so, and any strangers who had made that mistake had either ended up gut shot or gagging from a severed tongue.

Fortunately, he was able to stand with a minimum of effort that morning, although his bones ached and his muscles felt like they had been twisted in a dozen different directions in a fit of restless slumber. Before he could turn toward the campfire, he smelled the rich scent of coffee in the crisp morning air. Puzzled, he turned and was surprised to see a man sitting on the far side of the blaze. He was tall and lean, dressed in a black broadcloth suit and hat that had seen better days. He couldn't see his face. The fellow's head was bowed slightly, staring into the flames of the fire.

Warily, Otis walked toward him. His right hand found the curve of his pistol butt and rested there, ready to draw and fire, should the man have bad intentions. But the lanky fellow simply sat there, unconcerned that he had invaded the camp of thirteen of the deadliest outlaws west of the Mississippi. Otis looked toward the far side of the camp and saw the man's mount—a coal-black Morgan—standing where he had left him. It was a fine piece of horseflesh that would bring top dollar.

"Who the hell are you?" he demanded gruffly.

The man lifted his head and revealed his face. Just the sight of it gave Baker a start. The flesh was pale and shriveled, and the skin around his eyes—one gray and stone cold, the other milky yellow and blind—as well as his thin lips, was sickly blue in color. The cheeks of his narrow face were sunken and, amid the dark bristles of his eyebrows and mustache, Otis could see the plump, white bodies of maggots.

"Just a wayward traveler seeking a little companionship on the trail," was all that he said in reply.

"Good Lord Almighty!" exclaimed the one-armed man. "What's the matter with you, mister? Have you got a cancer or the consumption? You look five years past a churchyard burial!"

"I reckon I'm healthier than some and more worse for wear than others. I brewed a pot of coffee. Sit down a spell and have a cup."

Otis continued to the campfire. By the time he reached it, the other members of the Dozen were beginning to stir and leave their bedrolls. All seemed startled and perplexed at first, then grew suspicious of the man's presence, especially since he had apparently walked through the thick of them undetected. They drew their pistols and fetched rifles and shotguns, then joined their leader around the fire.

Otis Baker sat on a boulder and eyed the man on the other side of the flames. As the fellow poured from a coffee pot perched on stones amid the campfire and handed him a tin cup of tar-black coffee, he noticed two things he hadn't seen from a distance. One was a long-bladed Bowie knife with its point buried in the rocky earth next to the stranger's left boot. The other was a nickel-plated Colt Dragoon resting on the knob of his bony knee.

"You figuring to use that hogleg?" he asked sternly. "Maybe collect the bounty that's been placed upon our heads?" He took a sip of the coffee and darted his eyes to the others in his group. Two stood directly behind him, guns drawn, while four positioned themselves to the left and right, and the last two stood directly behind the tall visitor in the broadcloth suit.

"I have no want for money," he told him flatly. "Just stopped by to say howdy and brew this pot for the bunch of you." The stranger grinned slyly. "Besides, I'd be a damned fool to ride in here and take on thirteen desperados, don't you think?"

"The world's full of damned fools," Otis said, taking another drink. "You might be one of the unlucky ones."

The man opposite him stared him square in the face. "You see this here name etched on the barrel of my gun?"

Baker leaned forward and looked. "Missy? Who the shit is that? Some whore?"

The jaw muscles of the lean man's pale face tensed for a moment, but that ghoulish grin of his remained fixed and unwavering. "No. It's the name of a child we found stranded in the desert. Scarcely six years of age. Seems that a gang of bandits stopped her and her family down in Texas. Shot her pa square in the head, then violated her ma and sister, and did them in as well. A dreadful and unforgivable thing to do to an innocent child such as her."

Otis's eyes rose above the tall man's head and locked with the fellow standing directly behind him. In turn, the man drew a Remington revolver from his side holster and stepped up a ways, leaving barely a foot of space between himself and the stranger sitting before the campfire. In turn, the other members of Baker's Dozen cocked and levered pistols, rifles, and shotguns, their feet squared, ready to respond at a single nod from their commander.

"What's your intentions, you stupid son of a bitch?"

"I just came here to ask one question of you, Otis Baker," the man said. His voice was soft and calm... and as cold as frost on a winter pump handle.

The gang's leader chuckled. "And what would that be?" He smiled to himself, incredulous that the man would lead himself to the slaughter the way he had. Then he raised the tin cup to his lips and took another sip of coffee.

The grin on the stranger's face broadened, so much so that the flesh of his face stretched taut and creaked like old leather left in the sun far too long.

"Do you believe in angels?"

Midway through Otis Baker's last swallow of morning coffee, Dead-Eye lifted his hand. The .44 Dragoon was off his knee in a flash, cocked, and belching fire and gun smoke. The bullet angled upward, punched through the bottom of the tin cup, then tunneled through the roof of the outlaw's mouth and center of his brain. It exploded from the rear of his scalp in a blossom of blood, bone, and gray matter. Baker failed to twitch another muscle. He simply pitched forward and fell face first into the fire.

For many a day and night, Dead-Eye had studied the wanted poster he'd taken off the door of Ike Wheeler's livery stable in Socorro. Every face and the name that went with it was etched indelibly in his mind. The two behind Baker were Charlie Peterson and Gil McFadden. Dead-Eye lifted the muzzle of his Colt and put a round squarely through Peterson's breastbone, splitting the beating muscle of his heart clean in half. McFadden's Schofield pistol fired. The dead man's head rocked backward as the forty-five slug penetrated his cheekbone just below his right eye and exited from behind his ear. Dead-Eye fanned his hammer twice, placing one bullet in McFadden's throat and another between his eyes.

Before either man could hit the ground, Dead-Eye pulled the Bowie from the earth with his left hand. The man directly behind him, Buster Moon, fired directly into the back of his skull. The bullet tunneled downward through the center of his brain, then lodged in the meat of his tongue, halting only a quarter of an inch shy of his teeth. Dead-Eye coughed contemptuously and spat the wad of lead into the flames of the fire. Then, still in a sitting position, drove the blade of the knife backward. It entered the meat of Moon's leg just above the left knee. As the gunfighter rose to a standing position, he brought the honed edge of the Bowie up with him, cleaving open Moon's thigh and parting the wall of his femoral artery. Great gushes of crimson jetted from the open wound with each frantic beat of his heart.

The man's pistol went off a second time, puncturing Dead-Eye's left kidney. At the same time, a twelve-gauge shotgun to his right boomed. Buckshot opened a crater in the gunfighter's side, shattering four ribs and sending chewed innards through a second crater on the opposite side. The momentum of the blast turned Dead-Eye completely around. He brought the blade up and swept it cleanly across Buster Moon's gullet. The man dropped to his knees, his life's blood fast escaping through both his leg and his slit throat.

The man behind Moon was a half-breed Comanche named Joe Crow. He came at Dead-Eye with a knife of his own--an eight-inch skinner with a staghorn handle. The edge of Crow's blade went for the Southerner's throat, but grated across his collarbones instead. Dead-Eye drove his Bowie upward with a powerful thrust. The tip of its blade entered the flesh beneath the Indian's chin and emerged through the bridge of his nose. The man began to sputter and strangle as his sinuses became engorged with blood, which soon flooded his throat. Yanking the blade of the big knife free, Dead-Eye bore his weight forward as it went down. The edge parted Joe Crow's belly from sternum to groin. His entrails spilled forth and began to unravel at an alarming rate. His guts beat him to the ground as he fell.

A hail of bullets from revolvers and rifles assaulted Dead-Eye from the left. Several shattered his arm above and below his elbow, causing that appendage to become limp and useless. His fingers grew slack, releasing the haft of the big Bowie. A slug from a Winchester rifle punched through his upper thigh, breaking his femur clean in half. Unable to bear his weight, it collapsed beneath him. As he fell, Dead-Eye snapped off the final three shots from his Dragoon, taking down Big Mike Weston, Forrest Scott, and Avery Edwards. The fourth on his left, a young man scarcely eighteen years of age named Bailey Reed, lost his nerve and turned to run. Dead-Eye dropped the Dragoon and pulled Job's pepperbox pistol from the side pocket of his frock coat. He put one .36-caliber slug through the boy's spine and another in the back of his head as he dropped. For a split second he felt badly about shooting Reed in the back, but considering all the killing, stealing, and raping he'd been involved in, the gunfighter's regret was short-lived.

Bullets exploded from his right side and he rolled. He unloaded the rest of the pepperbox into a lanky fellow named Slim Sanders, then whipped the side of his coat aside revealing the sawed-down scattergun. Both hammers had been cocked before he had even entered the sleeping camp of the Baker's Dozen. He now pulled the triggers, expelling both loads from their muzzles. Two of the remaining three on the right—Cole Wagner and Austin Bennet—were blown bodily off their feet. They landed with a thud eight feet away, most of their midsections ripped away by a bee swarm of double-aught pellets.

As if in rebuttal, a single shotgun blast caught Dead-Eye in the right shoulder, dislocating his arm from the socket and turning it utterly useless.

Unable to stand or scarcely move at all, he lay on his back on the desert floor. The last standing man of the bunch—a big burly man with powder burns across his upper face named Blackie Price—stood over him, grinning like a jackass. One of the muzzles of his shotgun smoked from the spent shell, while the other was clear and open, ready to fire its second load. Dead-Eye watched grimly as the man lowered the scattergun, pressing the twin bores firmly against his forehead.

"You sorry, stinking son of a bitch!" Price gritted between rotten teeth. "Look at what you've done to Otis and the others!"

"I made a promise, so it had to be done." Dead-Eye's good eye narrowed and he smiled. "Besides… it's nothing to lose your head over."

Blackie Price thumbed back the second hammer and prepared to fire. But it never happened. Before he could pull the trigger, something grabbed hold of him by the nape of the neck, lifting him bodily from the ground. For a moment, he dangled there, kicking and screaming, his boots a good two feet off the earth. He felt strong teeth bear down on both sides of his neck, burrowing deeply, rending flesh and clamping onto the column of his neckbone. Then, with a fit of shaking and flailing, the thing that held him ended it all. His severed head went one direction and his lifeless carcass the other.

Dead-Eye looked up and saw Brimstone staring down at him. The demon horse's teeth grinned, coated with fresh blood.

"About time you showed up," grumbled the gunfighter. "Now, kneel down and see if you can nudge me onto your back. My work here is done, even if I did end up a mite incapacitated."

An hour later, Job and Missy met Brimstone as he crested the top of the ridge and rode into camp.

Dead-Eye laid limply across the saddle, his limbs twisted and turned in odd directions. As Job gently pulled him to the ground, they saw the extent of his injuries. They were too numerous to count with a single glance.

"You damned fool," rasped the mojo man beneath his breath.

Tears bloomed in Missy Slatter's eyes and spilled down her cheeks. "Oh, Mister Eye! They've done gone and shot you all to hell!"

"Don't cuss, Lil' Miss," Dead-Eye told her. He grinned reassuringly. "Besides, I'll be fit as a fiddle as soon as Job opens his bag of needles and thread and patches me up."

Job examined the broken man that lay stretched across the earth before him. "I'm afraid the damage is too great, son. I can plug up the bullet holes, but it looks like half the bones in your body are broken and splintered. There's nothing I can do about that a'tall. If there was a cemetery somewhere nearby, I could harvest the parts and do my best. But we're smack dab in the middle of the desert. There's no fresh bones to be found to mend you with."

Dead-Eye frowned sourly. "Well, now ain't that a turd in the stew pot."

"You shouldn't have done it, Mister Eye!" the child wailed. "Keeping the promise wasn't worth you being all broken and tattered the way you are!"

"I gave you my word and got it done, right down to the last man. It was worth it, child. You and your lost kin were avenged."

Suddenly, a look of hopeful inspiration shown in the girl's tearful eyes. She looked over at Job. "Use my pa's body! Take what you need and fix Mister Eye up, good as new!"

"No, ma'am!" Dead-Eye told her. "It was his wish to be laid to rest in the family plot."

A notion suddenly came to the mojo man. "I suppose we could use the remains of one of Baker's Dozen to repair you with."

But Missy was downright determined and unshakable. "You'll do nothing of the kind! It wouldn't be proper, filling my hero full of sinful bones like that! If I knew one thing about my pa, it was that he always paid his debts. He'd do anything possible to pay back anyone to which he was beholden. You did me and my family a great service. He would have been grateful for that and been proud to give of himself in order to square the balance of what he owed."

Job was impressed by the sacrifice the child was willing to make. "That would solve the problem. Her pa's body ain't in the best condition, but his bones are still strong and sturdy, and compatible in size. It'd take some doing, but I think I could make 'em work."

"Are you certain, Lil' Miss?" asked Dead-Eye, touched by the girl's offer.

Missy launched herself forward and hugged him tightly around the neck. "As sure as can be! Besides, how are you gonna get me all the way home to Holbrook if you're limp as a rag doll with your arms and legs all out of sorts?"

"All right then," agreed Dead-Eye gratefully. "I'm much obliged to you, girl." He looked over at Job, who stood appraising his damaged carcass. "I reckon you'd best get to work, old man. You've got to get me upright and able to straddle a saddle so we can ride back down to Baker's camp before nightfall."

"You're not intending to leave those hooligans there for the buzzards?"

"And forfeit five thousand in gold?" retorted Dead-Eye. "Hell no! Half of that bounty will serve as traveling money for our journey, while the other half will go to the girl's grandfolks for her upbringing and education. Besides, my pistol and your pepperbox are still down there, as well as that big-ass knife of mine. And I reckon you figured out this morning that I took your boiling pot and coffee grounds with me as bait for the trap."

"Yes," said Job with a disgruntled frown, "I surely did."

"Your favorite cup is down yonder, too," the gunfighter told him. "I'm sorry to say it suffered irreparable harm during the fray. But it served its purpose well and perished right honorably, if I do say so myself."

Chapter Thirteen

Holbrook
Arizona Territory
October 1870

Dead-Eye stepped out of the shop of J.N. Johnstone, Tailor & Clothier, on Holbrook's main street and stood upon the boardwalk for a long moment. Although it was officially autumn, the heat of a desert summer still lingered and the temperature was sweltering.

Out of curiosity, he turned and regarded his reflection in the store's windowpane. The new broadcloth suit he'd purchased was masterfully tailored and suited his frame well. The confrontation with Otis Baker and his men in the rocky hills of the Painted Desert had nearly destroyed him, but it had totally ruined his clothing beyond repair. The fresh black frock coat and britches, as well as a starched white shirt and string tie, made him appear more presentable and less deceased than he had looked before. The broadcloth material was stiff, but like thirst or hunger, he had no real need for comfort. Besides, a day or two on the trail and the garments would soften up and lose their newness. He'd be back to his dusty, grungy old self in no time.

He looked across the rutted dirt street and saw Job and Missy Slatter. The mojo man was handing a tall, silver-haired gentleman a bag of gold, Missy's share of the reward money for Baker's Dozen. The little girl was being smothered with hugs and kisses from a short, heavyset woman with equally silver hair. The grandparents.

Dead-Eye felt a dull ache down deep inside. He had fought tooth and nail to bring the child home to safety, but now that she was in her family's embrace, he couldn't help but feel a great sadness threaten to overcome him. He reckoned he'd gotten more attached to Missy and having her around than he'd suspected.

The grandfather, Elmer Slatter, shook Job's hand in appreciation. Dead-Eye figured that was the end of it, but he was mistaken. The elderly man looked across the street at him, then started his way.

Normally stoic and unphased, the Southerner found himself dreading the man's approach. *What the hell is he gonna make of me?* he found himself wondering. Different folks had different reactions to the fact that he was a dead man walking upright. Some seemed oblivious to the fact, while others accepted it without judgment. Some folks, however, found themselves confused and unnerved. He certainly didn't want Missy's grandfather to react negatively and drop dead of a heart attack or stroke smack dab in the street of his hometown.

Elmer Slatter seemed to have no such qualms, though. He stepped up on the boardwalk and extended a strong, calloused hand. Hesitantly, Dead-Eye shook it. The fact that he was as stiff as a clock spring and cold to the touch didn't appear to bother the man at all.

"Little Missy has told me all about you," the man said with a guarded smile. "I don't know exactly how you've become what you are or why. Being a Christian man, it goes against everything I've known or been taught. But I'm damned glad you found her out there in that godforsaken desert and was there for her when she needed you most."

"It's a grievous thing, what happened to your family," Dead-Eye replied. "Bringing her here to you was the decent thing to do. Most men would have done the same."

"Perhaps. But they wouldn't have ridden into the camp of the ones responsible and set things right. You've got this whole town talking... hell, the entire territory! You and your friend riding into town with the bodies of thirteen outlaws lashed to their horses... all stricken down by you alone, with only guns and a knife."

Dead-Eye nodded. "I figure most men couldn't have survived such. I only did so because of the way I am." He looked across the street and saw the little negro in the bowler hat talking to Missy and her grandmother. "I trust Job gave you Missy's share of the reward money."

"Yes," said Elmer. "It wasn't necessary, but it's appreciated nevertheless." The old man studied Dead-Eye for a long moment. "Missy told me of how my son's remains were made of use to you. I know my wife would rather have him buried back at the ranch, where she could visit and pray over his grave... but I have no objection to sharing him. James was a good, no-nonsense man with plenty of horse sense, heart, and backbone. But he wasn't always like that. Before he wed his Betsy, he was a hellraising man.

Spent a fair share of his time at the saloon, squandering his wages away on liquor, gambling, and whores. Many a night, he ended up in the town jail for busting some cowboy's skull in a fight or getting stinking drunk and shooting the windows out of the businesses hereabouts. It was only when he met that pretty little schoolmarm and settled down, did he cast aside those ways and found his true heart. Maybe that's what got him and most of his family killed in the end. He grew too complacent and trusting. If he'd still possessed the fiery temperament he'd shown in his youth, maybe Baker and the rest of those bastards wouldn't have gotten the drop on them."

"It's a hard land," the gunfighter admitted. "Many a good-natured man has fallen because of his kindness and grace. Sometimes, it's better to have a bit of rattlesnake beneath your skin when trouble comes calling."

Elmer Slatter thought to himself for a moment. "It may sound odd to say this, but I'm glad James was fortunate to have his second chance. Six feet beneath the earth, he's only a memory... as well as food for the worms and such. But using him the way you are, it gives purpose to his passing. It's sort of comforting, knowing that he's walking around inside you."

"A strange sentiment," Dead-Eye told him truthfully. "But I can't deny that I'm grateful. And, believe it or not, his bones have added a couple of inches to my frame."

Elmer laughed. "He always was a long-legged jackrabbit of a fella!" The old man's humor faded almost as quickly as it had begun, and he placed a strong hand on the gunfighter's shoulder. "I know you have a long, hard trail ahead of you. We'll be with you in spirit and prayer... particularly my granddaughter. She's taken quite a shining to you."

I'm right fond of her myself, he nearly said, but didn't. Dead-Eye simply nodded, shook the rancher's hand again, and watched him cross to the opposite side of the street.

Halfway there, Missy Slatter passed her grandpa and walked almost timidly toward the tall Southerner. "Howdy."

"Howdy," Dead-Eye said in return.

"I reckon you'll be leaving soon," she said. The girl avoided his eyes, looking down at the ground and kicking the dust of the street with the toe of her shoe.

"First thing in the morning," he replied. "Don't give Grandpa and Grandma any grief, you hear me? You're a handful and a half when comes to backtalking and snooping around. Mind your manners and behave yourself."

"Yessir." The girl's head remained bowed, looking at the earth at her feet. "I hope you find your boy soon."

"Me, too. That's why we can't linger. Gotta hit the trail and try to find him and the ones who made off with him."

Missy was silent for a moment longer. When she finally lifted her face, tears streamed down her rosy cheeks.

Dead-Eye knelt, took a handkerchief from his breast pocket, and made to wipe her eyes. Before he could, she rushed onto the boardwalk and wrapped her arms tightly around his neck.

"I don't know what I'm gonna do without you," she whispered in his ear. Her tears dampened the starched collar of his new shirt, but it wasn't an unwelcome sensation.

"Aw, don't carry on so, Lil' Miss," he told her softly. "Everything's all right. You're with folks who love you now."

"Don't you love me?"

That peculiar ache—reminiscent of the days when he had truly lived—haunted him from the pit of his chest. "You already know the answer to that question, child."

Missy hung onto him a while longer. "You know, when I get older and stout enough to hold a gun, I'm gonna learn to use it. Teach myself how to shoot straight and true... just like you, Mister Eye."

Dead-Eye nodded. "I think it's a good thing for a female to know how to handle firearms," he told her. "But I want you to promise you'll never use one for the wrong reason. Don't let what happened to your ma, pa, and sis rule your aim or your heart." For a second, the man felt ashamed. *Imagine me, of all people, giving her such advice.*

"I promise," she said. "Cross my heart and hope to eat flies." Missy released her hold and, taking the handkerchief offered her, wiped her eyes and blew her nose. She attempted to hand it back, damp and dripping with snot.

Dead-Eye looked at the soiled hanky. "No. You hold on to that for a keepsake."

The six-year-old nodded and did as she was told. She turned to leave, then whirled on her heels, and regarded him once again. "I ain't saying goodbye, you know."

"Then, I won't either." He nodded toward Elmer and Bess Slatter, who waited for her on the other side of the street. "Now, skedaddle."

Dead-Eye stood and watched as she joined her kin and climbed into a buckboard with them. As Elmer snapped the teams' reins, Missy waved to him as they drove past. The gunfighter in the black broadcloth suit and hat simply nodded and attempted to smile in reassurance. It was a dismal effort on his part.

"She'll be okay," Job told him as he crossed the street. "She's with her family now. Not trudging through the scalding hot wilderness with a couple of old, smelly drifters like us."

Dead-Eye said nothing in reply, for he knew his traveling companion was right. They'd done what they'd set out to do. Missy Slatter was no longer in danger. She could commence with being a normal, little girl again--playing hopscotch and Red Rover in the schoolhouse yard, baking cookies with her granny, and falling asleep in a warm, soft bed the way every child was meant to do.

"I do have some encouraging news, though," said the mojo man. "The sheriff who took those thirteen bodies off our hands told me that Jules Holland and his bunch was seen heading due west, no more than four months ago. So, it looks like we're getting closer to narrowing the distance between us and them."

"Then, we'd best prepare for the journey," said Dead-Eye. "Head over to the mercantile and buy supplies: coffee, tobacco, beans, whatever else you need. Maybe some more bailing wire and sewing thread for the next time you have to mend some bullet holes or reattach an arm or such. And, if you see silver of any kind, buy it. I'll take it to the gunsmith yonder and have him cast and load cartridges for the shooting irons we tote. If we're going up against unnatural foes once again, it's best to be prepared and loaded for bear."

"I agree," said Job. "I'll be back directly." The negro began to cross the street but stopped midway and turned. "You got that child safely back into the arms of her grandfolks. She'll grieve for a while, then learn to live with what happened." The lines of the black man's face softened a bit. "And so shall you."

As Job crossed the main throughfare of Holbrook, Dead-Eye turned his gaze toward the buckboard and its team of four mules. It kicked up a cloud of dust and grew smaller and less defined the further it traveled from town. Impassively, he stood there and didn't move a muscle until the wagon and its inhabitants gradually shrank away and was gone from sight. Then, he turned and, untying Brimstone and Balaam from a hitching post, started down the walkway to the livery stable, where the two animals would be fed and put up for the night.

Chapter Fourteen

Hellbound
Arizona Territory
November 1870

A s they rode across the arid expanse of central Arizona, Dead-Eye and Job came across a scattering of towns amid the desert wilderness. Most were made up of decent, God-fearing folks who had traveled and settled westward from the eastern half of the nation, usually for one of three reasons.

The first reason was that they were of an adventurous or optimistic nature, anxious to stake their claim in a vast new land that offered endless possibilities. The second, they had fled their homes back east because of the turbulent War Between the States or, if hailing from the South, the uneasy and reproachful Reconstruction that followed. The third reason was due to a hunger for gold, sparked by newspaper stories and dime novels declaring that the mountain streams and desert mines were brimming with treasure for the taking. Many a man had been snared by greedy ambition and many had died because of it. They either wasted away in cold water up to their knees, panning for gold that was nonexistent, and dying of exposure and lack of nourishment, so relentless was their obsession for unearned riches. Or they had ended up severely beaten or gunshot for the little gold they had actually discovered, which often didn't amount to enough to buy a swallow of cheap rotgut and a quick dance with a saloon girl.

Some would say that there was a fourth reason, one much darker, that had little to do with bettering one's prospects, at least as far as clean living and raising a family was concerned. It concerned men who desired to slip the bonds of lawfulness and moral responsibility. Many had been felons, drafted by the US government and released from Northern prisons to fight on the side of the blue, while others were disgruntled Southerners who had become cold-blooded guerilla fighters and bushwhackers during the conflict. Like Otis Baker, Garland Hughs, and other desperados Dead-Eye and Job had chanced across during their travels, these men chose to live without restraint or conscience.

As the two neared the far reaches of western Arizona, they were warned by well-meaning townsfolks and saddle tramps alike to avoid one town in particular. A town boasting more bloodshed and senseless slaughter than any in the territory. A town that drew the wantonly homicidal and the hopelessly deranged like blue bottle flies to rotting meat.

A town called Hellbound.

Needless to say, they ignored the warnings and soon found themselves entering the town's boundary from the east. They had been told several times, between Camp Lincoln and Hackberry, that Holland and his followers had stayed in the unsavory settlement for several days. Dead-Eye was convinced that someone in town might have information about where they had moved on from there. Job was more hesitant about pushing their luck, considering the town's reputation, but couldn't deny the fact that it could lead to a clue as to their whereabouts.

They arrived in late afternoon, with the western sun glaring down the rutted single street of the little township. There was something oddly disorienting and askew about the place. No structure seemed to be skillfully squared by level or plane, or even designed by architects who had the slightest idea of how to bring a successful building to a pleasing conclusion. The overhangs of porches hung low on one side and high on the other, and windows and doors seemed slightly misaligned. But that wasn't the only irregularity. The variety of paint hues used for embellishing the false-fronted structures was darker and more somber than what normal townspeople used. Dark grays, deep browns, and even midnight black covered the hotel, saloon, livery stable, and a dozen other points of commerce. Even in broad daylight, a perpetual pall of shadow seemed to engulf the community.

A sign over the doorway of a ramshackle barn at the edge of town read HELLBOUND LIVERY—HORSES & MULES—BOUGHT, SOLD, TRADED, BOARDED—WOODY McCLANAHAN, BLACKSMITH & SADDLERY SUPPLIER — WRANGLERS & SWINDLERS WILL BE SHOT TO HELL ON SIGHT!

"Right hospitable signage," Job observed as they reined to a halt outside the open doorway of the stable. "I wonder how he can discern agreeable clientele from no-account riffraff?"

Dead-Eye swung down from the black Morgan and swept the left side of his coat to the side, gaining access to the cross-holstered Dragoon, should he have need of it. "Maybe there ain't no agreeable clientele in this town," he said. Inside, he could hear the steely percussion of a mallet shaping horseshoes on an anvil. Rather than barge into the structure unannounced, the tall Southerner called into the gloomy interior. "Hey there! You've got paying customers out here!"

The hammer struck a couple more times, then halted. A moment later, the proprietor of Hellbound's only livery stable stepped into the sunlight, red-faced and perspiring profusely. With a scowl, he mopped his forehead with a bandana and wiped his massive hands on his leather apron. He was a big man, well over six and a half feet, and nearly half that wide in the shoulders. His hair and muttonchop whiskers were thick and unruly, and as orange as rusty barbwire. The thing that struck them most peculiar was the amount of armory he toted on his big frame as he labored. He wore twin Navy pistols on his hips, a double-barreled ten-gauge with a fancy sling across his broad back and a brace of long-bladed knives in crisscrossing sheaths across this barrel chest. The cutlery made Dead-Eye's Bowie look like a whittling knife in comparison.

"What the shit do you want?" he demanded suspiciously. The way he positioned his hands, he could have grabbed pistols, knives, or scattergun with equal speed and fluency.

"Hay and oats, as well as a couple of dry stalls for our animals," Job replied.

Woody McClanahan's eyes narrowed beneath his bushy brows. "What outfit are you with? I swear, if you've ever made off with a four-legged critter or put a questionable branding iron to dishonest use, I'd just soon cut you both in half with this here Clabrough and then haul you down the street to Miss Minnie's funeral parlor right here and now!"

"We're honest and square in our dealings," Dead-Eye told him flatly. "And, to tell the truth, if you attempted what you proclaimed, I'd likely blow off all ten of your fingers if you went for that ten-gauge, then shove it so far up your ass you'd taste gunpowder for a week."

McClanahan was surprised by the man's insolence. Something about the way he said it caused curiosity to override anger. He walked a few paces closer and studied the pair of travelers. Suddenly, he grinned. "Well, I'll be damned! Y'all come on in and I'll get you fixed up!"

As the man turned and walked back inside, Dead-Eye and Job took the reins of Brimstone and Balaam and followed. It seemed downright peculiar, the way the burly blacksmith had changed his tune all of a sudden.

McClanahan laughed. "Hell, I should've known it was you," he told Dead-Eye. "Folks hereabout know all about what you did on the far side of the territory. How you took down Otis Baker and his mangey bunch on your own. The Dozen have been through here a time or two, and everyone, even the hard-asses, were leery of bucking them or raising their ire. I reckon that's a shitload off some folks' minds now."

"News travels fast," said Job. "Did they write it up in a periodical or such?"

"Got wired here by telegraph," the liveryman explained. "I heard the fella in charge of the telegraph office in Holbrook sent the news all over the territory. You fellas are right famous… or infamous."

"It's nice knowing we're so well thought of," said Dead-Eye. He relieved the black horse of his saddle, led him into an empty stall, and then hefted his saddlebags over his shoulder.

"Well, I'd say that won't likely last for long. Particularly here in Hellbound. When folks find out you're here, I'd say they'll start lining up to test your mettle and give you a try."

"Wonderful," said Job with a shake of his head. "That's all we need. A bunch of greenhorn gunfighters aching to outdraw and plug you every minute we're here."

"You ain't gonna find no greenhorns here," the blacksmith told him grimly. "Every man in this town is a fair hand with a pistol. Some of them downright unnerving in their proficiency. If I were you, I'd especially steer clear of Creed and his bunch, the Hedgepath Brothers."

Dead-Eye had paid McClanahan for his services and was walking toward the street, when he froze in his tracks. His good gray eye narrowed as he slowly turned around. "Creed?"

"Yessir. Morgan Creed. Showed up here about two years ago. Meaner than a scorpion trapped in a lady's corset. Claims he was once a… "

"Prison guard, I'd fancy," Dead-Eye said. His voice was low and strangely venomous in nature.

"That's right," said the big man. "How did you—?"

Dead-Eye said nothing more, just turned and strolled out into the diminishing sunshine.

"Much obliged for finding a place for the critters, Mister McClanahan," Job told the livery man. "We'd be obliged if you'd keep an eye on our supplies and such. Don't want some no-account thief making off with them."

"Don't worry none about that! I bed down by the stall doors at night, to discourage such conduct. They'll be bled out and measured for a pine box before morning if they try to get past me."

"Is there a place in town with rooms for rent?" Job asked.

"There's a hotel called the Lotus Blossom a few doors down. It's run by a Chinaman by the name of Hung Lo. Not the cleanest place in Hellbound, but it'll do you for a night or two. Lo's not much to look at, kinda scrawny to tell the truth, but he's got a manner of fighting that folks around here steer clear of. I saw him break a man's neck with a fancy kick once… pert near took his head clean off. He runs an opium den in the basement, too, if you partake of such vices." McClanahan regarded the little mojo man for a moment. "Another thing you should take notice of. Trouble will likely hunt out your partner there, but you may end up finding your share as well. Those Hedgepath Brothers, they're dyed-in-the-wool rebs who refuse to bury the hatchet and are plumb loco to boot. They've horsewhipped or shot every man of dark complexion who's ridden through this town, even hanged a couple on occasion. So, you'd best watch your back and take care."

"I appreciate the warning," Job said, tipping his bowler. Then he canted the Henry rifle over his shoulder and joined Dead-Eye outside.

When he got there, he noticed a wicked little smile on the zombie's pale face.

"What's got you grinning like a briar-eating mule?" the negro asked him.

"Morgan Creed."

Job rolled his eyes in exasperation. "I do declare! Every time some hombre's name rolls off your tongue like that, they end up dead in the worst sort of way. Who in tarnation is this Creed anyhow?"

"I'm thinking you'll find out soon enough," Dead-Eye simply told him.

Together, they walked down the middle of the dirt street, surveying their surroundings. The further they traveled, the more apparent it was that Hellbound was well deserving of its name and reputation. The boardwalks and walls of the surrounding buildings seemed to be stained with dark splatters and rivulets of dried blood, as well as clinging bits of tissue that had been forfeited by their unlucky victims. Bullet holes and buckshot pits were plentiful in the porch railings and hitching posts, evidence of the violence that was common within the town limits. Forgotten beneath a rocking chair in front of a gunsmith shop was a severed hand still clutching a Colt revolver. Green flies buzzed around the stump of the decaying member, perpetuating their colony with pulsing maggots in the ragged, rotten meat.

The town's funeral parlor was located directly across the street. The sign over the doorway read MINNIE GRAVES—MORTICIAN—EMBALMING, DISPLAY, & INTERMENT—CASKETS FOR SALE OR RENT. Out front of the blackwashed storefront were a couple of heat-bloated bodies propped up in vertical coffins constructed of yellow pine. On one of the men, who had been shot squarely in the forehead, was pinned a crudely-lettered sign that read DO YOU KNOW THIS MAN? Apparently, the poor fellow had met his demise and no one in town claimed him or knew who the hell he was.

A lean woman in her forties with mousy brown hair and spectacles walked outside and began sweeping the boards of the causeway. She was dressed oddly, in a man's high-collared shirt, bowtie, and dark pants. The woman noticed them and stopped her tidying for a moment.

"Pardon me!" she called out to Dead-Eye. "Lazarus! Do you know this poor gent here?" She nodded toward the corpse with the sign on his chest.

"No," the gunfighter replied. "Should I?"

Minnie Graves shrugged her narrow shoulders. "Being of the same celestial realm, I figured you might have run into him in the afterlife. In any event, I'm owed payment for services rendered." She smiled lustily and winked. "Just thought if you were his kin, you might pay off the debt, either with gold or a more amorous transaction of mutual benefit."

"Maybe you don't need to walk all the way to the hotel after all," said Job. "Miss Graves might have a bed for you over there. You should feel right home, propped up betwixt those two."

"Nonsense!" she replied. "He can spend the night in my quarters. Wouldn't be the first time I've shared a bed—or a slab—with the dead." Then, laughing, she finished her chore and went inside.

The little mojo man was impressed. "A necromancer in the truest sense. I'd not judge you if you decided to take her up on her offer."

"A female undertaker?" mused Dead-Eye. "And decked out in men's britches, besides! I don't believe I've ever come across such before."

"I reckon a woman has the right to do what she sees fit to survive in a town like this, either servicing horny outlaws or attending to the dead."

Soon, they were entering the two-story structure of the Lotus Blossom Hotel. The place had a musky, ill-kempt smell to it, which mingled with a strong floral odor that Job recognized as essence of poppy. They stepped up to the boardinghouse's front desk where a short, lean man of Oriental heritage stood, dressed in a dark *changshan* tunic and skull cap. Sensing their presence, he looked up from a stack of gold coins and an abacus, and regarded them blandly.

"May I assist you gentleman?"

"Are you Hung Lo?" asked Dead-Eye.

The Asian cocked an eyebrow and smiled. "That's what the ladies tell me." Then, amused by the cleverness of his humor, he cackled loudly to himself.

The gunfighter and the mojo man looked at one another wearily, then Job proceeded. "We're in need of a room, not a smart-ass landlord."

"I can certainly accommodate your needs," Hung Lo told them, taking no offense. "Three dollars for a night's stay in a room upstairs, or five for a cot downstairs."

"Kinda expensive to sleep in a dank cellar, don't you think?" said Dead-Eye.

The Chinese man reached beneath the counter and pushed a couple of long-stemmed clay pipes toward them. "The latter comes with these and all the black dragon you wish to consume."

Job took three gold pieces from a vest pocket and laid them on the counter before the man. "We'll take our boarding upstairs, if you please. I'm more of a drinking than smoking man. Particularly of the type of tobacco you peddle."

Hung Lo shrugged. "Suit yourselves." The opium pipes disappeared as swiftly as they had appeared. "Don't judge me for my chosen trade. A man of my race, in a town such as this, tends to last as long as a fart in a high wind. Iniquity and vice are desirable commodities in Hellbound, and so I provide its residents with what they desire. And, in turn, they leave me be."

"Can't condemn a man for saving his earnings and his skin at the same time," said Dead-Eye.

"Truthfully, I am considered the black sheep of my family. My half-brother, Hop Sing, resides in Nevada and works honestly as a cook for a white rancher and his three sons. Grown-ass men and still living with their daddy. Bunch of losers!" The hotel owner slid a skeleton key across the counter. "Room Eight, upstairs at the end of the hallway. And, if you have a problem with the rats and cockroaches, take it up with them. They were there before you."

"Much obliged," said Job. He took the key, looking as though he didn't mean it as much as he ought to.

On the way up the narrow staircase, Dead-Eye glanced over his shoulder at the little black man. "Must be a trying thing, being harassed and put upon because of the color of your skin all the time."

"Seems to me you kept some of us bound in chains before the War abolished that wretched practice," Job replied. "I know it may have been how you were raised and such, but that never made it decent or right."

The Southerner nodded. "I can't deny that you're correct. Considering my change of heart following that profane conflict, I wish I'd undone my father's offense and granted them their freedom a long time ago." As they reached the second floor, he regarded his traveling partner. "What do you propose we do now?"

"Let's leave our gear in our room, then head to the saloon across the street," Job suggested. "We came here for answers concerning those we seek, and I reckon that'd be the best place to begin."

"And, while you're there, you intend to imbibe in a shot of whiskey or two, I suppose."

The mojo man grinned. "Good news or bad, a little fire in the furnace makes it easier to celebrate or bite the bullet, whichever it may be."

Chapter Fifteen

The Poisoned Waterhole
Hellbound
November 1870

By the time they stepped out onto the street again, twilight had begun to fall. To the west, the sunset painted the open sky with broad strokes of crimson and purple. Just casting one's eyes upon it gave a vague premonition of dark times ahead.

They crossed the street to the saloon. From within the building could be heard rowdy laughter, the clinking of beer mugs and shot glasses, and off-key piano playing. Before they stepped up on the boardwalk, the two glanced up at the sign nailed over the eaves of the overhang. It read THE POISONED WATERHOLE SALOON.

"Well, that's a mighty comforting name for a drinking establishment," said Dead-Eye.

"Maybe to you," Job told him. "But then, you're not the one who's going to be doing the drinking, are you?"

"Don't see any hostile signs barring you from entering, so I reckon you're safe to go in."

"I suppose we'll find out when I walk up to the bar." The gunfighter started toward the door, but Job took hold of his arm, halting him before he could enter. "Remember, we're going in here to ask questions and get answers. No getting your back up and killing half the folks in the place, no matter how ornery they might be. I know that's like asking a catfish to fly to the moon and back, but at least put some effort into trying. Alright?"

Dead-Eye smiled. "I'll be a perfect gentleman."

"Maybe when you were alive. But ever since I snatched you from the bony fingers of death and set your feet back in the mortal world, you've been as unpleasant and contrary as a mangy mountain lion with a winter-long toothache and a rash upon his balls."

A moment later, they were though the doorway and inside The Poisoned Waterhole. The place was lit up with coal oil lanterns hanging from chandeliers fashioned from old wagon wheels. The illumination they cast was muted by a heavy pall of tobacco smoke that hung throughout the big barroom, nearly as thick as a morning fog. The place stank of hand-rolled cigarettes, liquor, and unwashed men. It reeked of unwashed women as well. The second floor was open overhead, and along the railing of the upstairs landing sat eight or nine painted ladies decked out in lacy corsets, silk bloomers, and black stockings. The strumpets waited patiently for the men below to get their fill of hooch and poker, and come looking for more pleasurable activity.

Dead-Eye sniffed at the air. "Speaking of catfish," he said, nudging the little man beside him.

"I told you to behave yourself," Job snapped beneath his breath. "Now, come on."

As the two walked toward the long mahogany bar, they surveyed their surroundings and those who congregated there. All looked to be hard men molded by luckless desperation and lacking common morals and decency. As they indulged in strong drink and wagered over games of chance, they laughed and bragged about how many men had fallen brutally to guns, knives, and fists. No hesitancy or shame girded their lips as they boasted of cut throats, bullet-riddled skulls, gutted bellies, or severed genitals.

When Dead-Eye and Job reached the drinking counter, the negro knocked on the scarred surface, drawing the attention of the bartender. The man—as bald as a doorknob and scarecrow thin—left a conversation at the end of the bar and walked to where they stood.

"What'll it be?"

"A beer and a whiskey," Job told him. "And the best you have. Not some watered-down horse piss."

The barkeep turned his eyes to Dead-Eye. "How about you?"

"Nothing for me," the Southerner simply said.

"A place at the bar is for drinking, not taking up space like a teetotaling son-of-a-bitch."

The gunfighter lifted his head a couple of inches, staring the bartender square in the face, one eye gunmetal gray, the other wide and casting an unnerving glow. "I told you, I wasn't thirsty."

The look on Dead-Eye's face warned the bartender to refrain from pushing the matter. He left and, returning with a filthy mug of beer and a shot glass of amber liquor, set it in front of Job. The mojo man slapped a coin on the counter, then took a swallow from the beer mug. He grimaced sourly. "You sure that *you* didn't pull out your pecker and piss in this glass?"

The bartender grinned with rotten teeth. "If I had, you'd be well deserving of it, you burr-headed, little nigg—"

Before the sentence could be completed, Job leveled a dark finger at the fellow. "You allow that offensive word to cross your lips and, I swear, I'll cast a hoodoo on you that'll waste you away to the bone before sunrise. They'll find you in your bed, shriveled up and at death's door. Your own feeble granny could tote you to the grave in a picnic basket, you'll be so scrawny and lacking."

"Don't doubt that he can't do it, either," Dead-Eye told him. "Those charms and doo-dads around his neck ain't no young'un's play-pretties. That's some serious swamp magic around his throat."

The bartender studied the odd collection of talismans that dangled from the black man's neck. From several lanyards and chains hung the feathers of an eagle, a buzzard, and an owl, three tiny bottles of colored glass, a link of gator teeth, and the dried foot of a rooster. From the guarded expression on his lean face, it was apparent that he had a good idea what sort of mischief and misery the jujus could conjure.

"Aw, the hell with you!" he grumbled, then turned and walked back to the far end of the bar.

"I thought we weren't gonna raise a stink in here," Dead-Eye said. "Kinda looks like you're making a point of it."

Job glared at the barkeep's back as he returned to serving drinks. "You know how that word hackles my hide."

As the two stood there, the mojo man drinking and the zombie simply standing and biding his time, uproarious laughter erupted from a table in the corner furthest from the front door. Dead-Eye lifted his head and studied the bunch in the reflection of a cloudy mirror hanging behind the bar. Three big, rawboned fellows in filthy cotton shirts and woolen britches sat there, smoking cigarettes and drinking. They wore no hats and, from a distance, their heads looked oddly askew and misshapen. The fourth man at the table was a massive, black-bearded fellow smoking a cigar. He was decked out in a faded blue officer's coat and a high-peaked, flat-brimmed hat of black felt. The man's cruel eyes were aimed directly at Dead-Eye's back with an intensity that would have bored holes through his flesh and bone if they'd possessed the power to do so.

"Boys, have I ever told you of a sorry piece of shit I had custody of during the last year or so of the War?" he asked boisterously, making sure his voice carried clearly throughout the barroom. "His name was Wingade. A soft, prudish man who was raised with a silver spoon in his mouth and his daddy's cotton-growing money wiping his prissy ass since the day of his birth. He wasn't much to begin with, but he became much less in my hands. It was a damn pleasure tormenting that bastard every hour of every day... beating him within an inch of his miserable life and turning his soul inside out. When he was released after the War, he crawled out of that prison camp, shaking and shivering like a man three times his age!"

The three others at the table rocked back in their chairs and cackled uproariously at the story that was told. In the mirror, the smile of the big man in the Union greatcoat broadened considerably.

Job didn't turn his head. Just took a long sip of whiskey and sighed, knowing things could very well turn sour fast. "That feller the livery man spoke of. Creed. Is that him?"

Dead-Eye nodded. "It is." Slowly, he pushed away from the bar and turned. Sensing Job's frustration, he laid his mind to rest. "Don't worry none. I'm only going over to pay my respects to an old friend. I ain't intending to do anything to start a ruckus."

"You never do," said the black man, turning back to his drinking. "It just seems to cut loose like a randy bull after a heifer's hindquarters."

Dead-Eye walked leisurely through the tightly-packed barroom, moving between the tables, heading toward the one in the far corner. The man named Morgan Creed watched him the entire time, his smile unwavering. Then, through the grayish-blue pall of tobacco smoke, the Southerner's features grew clearer and Creed's smirk slipped a notch or two. As Dead-Eye reached the table, the big man's eyes widened with growing alarm.

"Well, I declare!" he rasped. "What the shit happened to you, Wingade?"

The tall man with the pale and sunken face simply stood there and studied the four with his mismatched gaze. Morgan Creed appeared much the same as he had when he had proven himself to be the cruelest and most sadistic guard at Camp Chase. It was the other three men who interested him to a larger degree. Up close, he could tell that they were brothers, due to their build and the color of their hair. But something had gone terribly wrong with them sometime in their lives. Their features were gruesomely twisted, their heads cocked at odd angles on their crooked necks, and nasty scars ran like railroad lines on a map across their skulls from base to forehead, and across from ear to off-centered ear. The most unnerving thing about them were their eyes. A maniacal glee seemed to shine from within the orbs, caring for nothing or no one. Only the desire to inflict pain and violence.

"I'm dead, is what," Dead-Eye told the bearded man, his voice winter cold and as smooth as a whore's caress. "I died shortly after I left that vile hellhole back in Ohio. Just thought I'd come back from Hell to haunt your foul and spiteful ass."

Morgan Creed chewed on the butt of the cigar in the corner of his mouth. His eyes went to the big forty-four Dragoon pistol angled across the gaunt Southerner's midsection, then to the bony, bloodless hand that hung limply at his side. It was deathly still with nary a tremble to it at all.

The three men at Creed's table eyed the stranger who faced their boss and slowly began to stand. Their hands were already fisted around their holstered pistols, ready to draw.

"Sit your asses down," the bearded man told them. They hesitated for a long moment, then their wild eyes seemed to glaze over with bewildered frustration. When they were back in their chairs, he looked up at the specter of the man he had once humiliated and tortured. "Have you come to kill me, Wingade?"

"Hell, I didn't even know you were here until I rode into town," the Southerner told him. "And I no longer go by my former name. That was a life and death ago. Now, folks just call me Dead-Eye."

The three freakishly scarred brothers looked at one another. "Shitfire! That's the one who—"

"I've heard of what he did!" snapped Creed. His eyes never left his adversary's pale and mustachioed face. "So, is that it? Are you aiming to collect a bounty on our heads as well?"

A narrow smile crept across Dead-Eye's blue lips. "Why would a corpse have a need or desire for money? If I decide to kill you, it'll be for personal gratification."

Morgan Creed's broad face paled a shade or two. "If you're intending to do so, it'll have to wait. It's growing late and we have business to attend to." He dug into the fob of his vest to withdraw his pocket watch. Before he could do so, a crisp *ca-click* sounded in his ears and he noticed that Dead-Eye's hand was laid across the curved butt of the Dragoon, his thumb perched on the cocked hammer. A split second before, it had dangled at his side with no clear intention of moving.

Nervously, Creed attempted to swallow, but could conjure no spit to do so. "Just fetching my timepiece." He withdrew the watch by its chain and flipped it open with his thumb. The time was nearing nine o'clock. "Let's go, boys," he said to the trio of brothers. As he stood, he regarded Dead-Eye warily. "You just riding through or do you intend to stick around?"

"I'll be here only as long I need to be," the dead man told him. "See you around, Creed."

The former prison guard said nothing in reply. He simply motioned to the others to follow and headed for the saloon door.

A moment later, Job was standing next to him. "I'd say that took a measure of restraint on your part."

Dead-Eye's pale face still held the unnerving smile he had subjected Morgan Creed to. "Much more than you could imagine." He eased the hammer down on his pistol and allowed his hand to slip to his side. When he looked at Job, he saw a twinkle in the negro's dark brown eyes. "What are you so damn cheerful about?"

"I believe I've found someone who can provide answers for those questions we've been wanting to ask," he told him. "And you'll never believe who it is!"

Without further hesitation, Dead-Eye followed Job through the crowded barroom to the staircase that led to the upper floor. Once they got there, they found a man waiting for them. He was elderly, perhaps in his mid-seventies, but ramrod straight and tall. His hair was silver in color and an equally hued mustache graced his upper lip, the tips ending below the corners of his mouth. On the breast of his charcoal-gray coat was pinned a brass star with the words U.S. MARSHAL engraved in the metal and around his narrow waist was a tanned gun belt baring a brace of Colt revolvers with mother-of-pearl grips.

There was no doubt whatsoever in Dead-Eye's mind as to who the stately gentleman truly was. "I'll be damned," he said, a trace of awe in his gravelly voice. "If it ain't J.B. Hill in the flesh!"

John "Boot" Hill was a legend of law and order known not only throughout the western territories, but east of the Mississippi River as well. Many a boy had idolized the larger-than-life lawman after reading dime novels of his heroic exploits, written by the likes of Ned Buntline, Edward Ellis, and Prentiss Ingraham . If one could believe what they read, Boot Hill had single-handedly battled marauding Indians and brought countless outlaws to judgment, either from bullets or at the end of a hangman's noose.

The lawman stood with a buxom, red-haired woman of fifty or so years—much older than the young girls positioned around the upstairs landing, waiting to be chosen or called for service. "Miss Flossie," he told her, "I need to speak to these two gentlemen, alone, without spying eyes or prying ears about."

The madam nodded and clapped her manicured hands loudly. "Ladies! Let's give Marshal Hill and his guests here a little privacy, shall we?" With that, the prim and painted whores retired to their designated rooms, and Miss Flossie to her parlor a few doors away.

"We don't get many visitors here in Hellbound... at least not of a decent nature," the marshal told them. "Most folks who ride through do just that, and don't linger to tempt their fate."

"We've come to ask a few questions," Job told him, "concerning the whereabouts of Jules Holland and his followers."

Boot Hill nodded gravely. "I know of whom you speak. They're not here, but they were a few months ago. It was a dark time, it was, even for an evil place like this. Holland *recruited* a couple of Flossie's girls, who bit and cursed a dozen or more of the Waterhole's patrons in turn. I enlisted the assistance of Woody McClanahan down at the livery stable and, together, we hunted out the bloodsucking fiends and staked them through their hearts. It was a brutal, fearsome matter, but we got it done."

"So, you're accustomed to such supernatural dealings?" asked Dead-Eye.

"If you've traveled the miles I have and encountered the number of folks I've crossed paths with over the years, you tend to run into an unholy thing or two in your time. Vampires are the more common of the bunch." The lawman regarded the pale Southerner with a wry smile. "Zombies are a sight rarer."

Job was quiet for a moment, then he asked a question that had been nagging him. "Was there a negro woman and a young boy with them?"

"There was," replied Hill. "And I was glad to see her get in that black wagon of hers and leave with the rest." A troubled look shone in the law-man's eyes. "One night, four men here at the saloon got liquored up and decided they'd pay her a visit and have their way with her. The next morn-ing, every last one of them were found spiked to cactuses at the edge of town, their eyes gouged from their skulls and their arms and legs ripped completely off. Mind you, I said *ripped* off, not cut."

"And the boy?" asked Dead-Eye.

"More of a young man than a boy. Tall and gangly, with dark hair. Resembled you in a way." The elderly man detected a somber look in the gunfighter's good eye. "I take it that wasn't a coincidence."

"It was his son Daniel," Job told him. "He was abducted by Holland and his gang years ago."

"Well, he kept close to Holland, that was for sure... like a son to a father." Hill paused, as though wondering if he should mention some-thing. "This might be hurtful to hear, but I only saw the two of them out and about at nighttime. Never in broad daylight."

"Any idea where they were headed after they left Hellbound?"

"They rode due north. I heard they were headed for Wyoming terri-tory." The marshal regarded Dead-Eye. "I know who you are. Both of you. The tale of what you did to avenge that poor child... it's spread all over the territory. Otis Baker and his dozen were an immoral and dastardly crew. I'm much obliged to you for dispatching them the way you did. Much less worry for me and other folks here in town, decent or otherwise."

"No big deal. It was a promise that needed to be kept."

"I saw you down there talking to Morgan Creed and the Hedgepath boys. What was your business with them?"

A cruel grin crossed the gunfighter's face. "Let's just say Creed and I have a history. As for those boys, I've never seen them before tonight."

"They're brothers," Boot Hill told him. "Named Cain, Abel, and Seth. Their folks were either of a biblical frame of mind, or they had a wicked sense of humor."

"What's wrong with them anyhow? Are they deformed or deranged?"

"I'd say plenty of both. The way I've heard it, they served in an artillery brigade under General Hood. During the Battle of Chickamauga, the fighting grew so fierce that the one who was in charge of loading their cannon mistakenly rammed two cannonballs into the bore rather than one. When they touched it off, the artillery piece exploded and nearly tore all three of their heads off. They were taken to a doctor in town who had a questionable reputation for dabbling in medical practices and experiments that blasphemed in the face of God Himself. They called him the Mad Doctor, as well as other less polite monickers. He operated on those boys' brains, removing the damaged pieces and replacing them with parts from dogs and wild critters. Whatever he did, he stripped away every last trace of decency and restraint from them. I'd say they've killed more men, locals and strangers, than any twelve men here in Hellbound. Plus, that eccentric sawbones stitched their faces and heads together in a way that made them look more like monsters than men."

"If they've killed so many, why haven't you locked them up or hanged them?" asked Dead-Eye. "You're the town marshal, ain't you?"

Hill laughed uneasily. "If I were to arrest and jail every man who shot, knifed, or beat a pour soul to death hereabouts, I'd be stacking them in the cells like cord wood. Best to just keep them within the town limits and let them whittle each other down, one by one."

The tall Southerner glanced over at Job. He could see by the look in the black man's face that he was as troubled by the man's words as he was.

"It's good that Creed has some sort of peculiar hold over those three. If he didn't, they'd probably have killed you before you reached their table. Or at least tried their best." The marshal eyed the dead man in the black suit. "With their help, Creed has forged a reputation as a stage robber and rustler in the territory. Truthfully, he's a poor hand with a gun. That's why he keeps the Hedgepaths around. However, he does have an unhealthy fascination with explosives. A month ago, a crate of dynamite was stolen from a silver mine a few miles north of here. I'd say he was responsible for its disappearance."

"It sounds like the man," said Dead-Eye. "Cruel and destructive in every way imaginable."

"Tell me this… do you intend to kill Creed before you leave town?"

"If anyone in this world deserves it, he does," the gunfighter said and left it at that.

"If you decide to, I won't find fault in you. Those four polecats fear and despise me. They've been gunning for me for a while now. Their banishment from this town, or life itself, would certainly ease my mind."

Following their meeting with Boot Hill, Dead-Eye and Job made their way back down the staircase to the barroom below.

"So, did your assessment of the good marshal and his dedication to his position—or lack of—match mine?" Job asked with a frown.

"He sure wasn't the lawman depicted in those dime novels I read while fighting in the War," Dead-Eye declared. "I reckon that old saying about never meeting your heroes face to face is true, particularly in his case."

Chapter Sixteen

The Lotus Blossom Hotel
Hellbound
November 1870

The moment they stepped out of The Poisoned Waterhole and onto the street, they sensed that the dark and dangerous hours of the town named Hellbound had begun to commence. Sinister sounds echoed through the dark side streets and alleyways, causing their nerves to heighten and their hands to stay within reach of their firearms. Shrill screams of terror and low moans of pain and agony, the meaty thud and crack of clenched fists upon flesh, numerous gunshots from pistol, rifle, or shotgun... all assaulted their ears as they made their way toward the Lotus Blossom. Anywhere else, such severe and violent noises would have been unthinkable. On the streets of that Arizona settlement, they were as commonplace as the chirring of crickets or the lonesome call of a nightbird.

They were halfway across the avenue when a foul odor, or combination of such, assaulted their nostrils.

"Do you smell that?" asked Dead-Eye. The stench was nearly unbearable, but not unfamiliar. "The stink of bloated and decaying bodies, of gangrene and infected flesh, and the offensive air of a battleground's infernal aftermath."

Job halted in his tracks and scowled. "For me it's the swampy smell of rotten vegetation and stagnant water rife with sickness and disease. Freshly-spilled blood and guts torn asunder, reeking of bile and shit."

Dead-Eye shucked his pistol from its holster and held it at the ready. "I reckon you know who usually shows up in the midst of such nastiness."

A deep chuckle echoed from the shadows between the hotel and an abandoned building. A pair of eyes and a broad, toothy grin blazed crimson with an inner heat in the darkness. "Howdy, gents. It's been a while."

As Dead-Eye cocked his forty-four, Job drew the pepperbox pistol from his vest pocket. Both stood stone still and faced what was to come, knowing good and well in the back of their minds that their weapons were currently loaded with common lead and not silver.

A form stepped from the gloom and revealed itself before them. It was a man, tall in stature and lean of muscle. His face was handsome and clean-shaven, and his long, raven-black hair lay lank across his broad shoulders. He wore a long, knee-length coat that gleamed in the glow from the saloon windows like the scaly hide of a black snake. Around his hips was a gun belt sporting twin revolvers of unknown make and origin. The pistols seemed to glow a muted red in their holsters, like irons hot and ready for branding. Although the sleeve of the ebony coat concealed it, Dead-Eye and Job knew the length of the stranger's right arm, from shoulder to fingertips, was embellished with an elaborate tattoo that made the entire appendage resemble a poisonous green viper.

"John Legion," hissed the cadaverous gunfighter beneath his breath. Dead-Eye faced the man, aware that his third confrontation with the otherworldly bounty hunter could prove disastrous compared to the previous two.

"You are unprepared... both of you. You should know by now that I can sense the presence of silver. I still carry a fragment of that accursed metal in my back from our last encounter." He smiled, his long teeth wolf-like and full of menace. "You have no need for worry, though. I haven't come for you this time, but for someone else."

"And who would that be?" Job asked.

"I'm not at liberty to divulge that fact," Legion answered. "That's between me and the one who hired me."

"Why do you tell us this, if it doesn't concern us?" Dead-Eye wanted to know.

"Because, when the time comes, I want no interference from you. I know how damned stubborn and trigger-happy you can be. At the hour of reckoning, you must step aside and allow me to ply my trade in the way I see fit."

"And if it turns out to be someone undeserving of your wrath?"

"Oh, they are most certainly deserving, I assure you that. Now, you must promise me that you will stand down and refrain from impeding my mission."

The zombie shook his head. "I cannot commit to such a vow... not until I see with my own eyes who you intend to strip of their soul and drag to Hell."

John Legion's smile faded. His eyes blazed red hot like coals from a smithy's furnace. "If that be the case, then you'd best be loaded with silver and shoot straight and true. If not, I shall destroy you."

"I thought that was your intention all along," Job declared. "At the urging of my daughter, Evangeline."

Legion was amused. "Oh, don't worry. That contract still stands. But there is a time for the execution of every transaction… and your time is yet to come." The tall man in the snakeskin coat settled his gaze on Dead-Eye's gaunt face. "Heed my warning, living dead. Mind your own business and allow me to accomplish mine when the time comes." Then, without warning, he stepped backward and was instantly swallowed by the void of night.

Dead-Eye and Job stood in the center of the street for a long moment, rattled by their sudden encounter with the bounty hunter named Legion. "Who do you suppose he's been sent to dispatch?" asked the Southerner.

"In an evil town like this, there is no telling," Job replied. "I'd say there are dozens, maybe hundreds of men within a stone's throw that is deserving of Legion's brand of fiendish justice."

Dead-Eye considered something. "You don't think it could be Boot Hill he's after?"

"I'm afraid to admit it, but that could very well be," allowed the little mojo man. "A man like him makes countless enemies during his lifetime. I wouldn't put it past most of them being willing to sell their very soul to assure that he pays for whatever wrong they believe he has done to them, be it justified or otherwise."

In the darkness of Room Eight of the Lotus Blossom Hotel, Dead-Eye sat in a cane-backed chair in the center of the room, silent and lost in his own thoughts. Due to the fact that he was physically deceased, his heart failed to beat and his lungs neglected to breathe in the stale air of the hotel room. His mind still functioned, however. It was because of that state of dual existence that he was cursed to relive trauma and heartache over and over again, unrestrained by the true numbness of death.

Job slept peacefully in the room's brass-framed bed. The mojo man snored loudly, as he was accustomed to, sounding like a dull-toothed crosscut saw attempting to cut into the rigid column of a hickory tree.

Shortly after midnight, someone from a neighboring room began to pound on the wall. "Quiet down, damn you!" growled a man's voice from the other side.

Job muttered in his sleep, snorted, then continued his snoring.

A minute passed, then the voice came again. "I said SHUT THE HELL UP!"

And, with that, a single gunshot rang out.

The bullet tunneled through faded wallpaper, plaster, and wood, and erupted into the cool darkness of Room Eight. By chance, the projectile struck Dead-Eye in the right temple, bore through the sluggish mass of his moldering brain, and exited through the opposite side.

Jolted from his sleep, Job sputtered and sat upright in bed. "What the shit was that?"

"A confounded bullet going through my skullbone," Dead-Eye told him. The tall Southerner stood and shook his head, attempting to rid himself of a ringing in his ears. As a result, the sludge of his blackened brain splashed across the wall of the hotel room. Incensed, he started for the door.

"Where are you going?"

"I intend to give the son of a bitch a piece of my mind!"

"Looks like you've done that already," said Job, climbing out of the feather bed. The mojo man tugged on his britches and slipped his suspenders over his shoulders. "Hold up and I'll go with you."

A moment later, Dead-Eye was in the hallway, knocking on the door of Room Seven. Abruptly, the door was wrenched open and the room's occupant glared at the two. The man was of average height with unruly dark hair and a clean-shaven face. He was clad only in woolen underwear and held a long-barreled Smith & Wesson Russian revolver with ivory grips in one hand. The muzzle was still smoking from the shot that had been fired.

"What do you want?" he snapped, thoroughly pissed off.

"I'm the fella you shot at through the wall," Dead-Eye told him with irritation.

"Well, hell, you had it coming," the man said. "You were snoring loud enough!"

"I was the one doing the snoring," Job informed him. "He just received the brunt of your frustration."

The dark-haired fellow examined the wounds in Dead-Eye's head. "Damn, mister! Most folks I shoot stay dead. You're the first cadaver who ever hunted me down and knocked on my door." He thumbed back the hammer of his forty-four pistol and smirked. "Maybe I oughta remedy that right here and now!"

Before the man could aim and fire, a door across the hall opened. "What in tarnation is all the ruckus?"

They turned to find Boot Hill standing there, dressed in a long night-shirt with his twin-holstered gun belt buckled around his waist. The law-man's silver hair stood up in a half-dozen cowlicks. Behind him stood Miss Flossie, holding a bedsheet around her generous bosom to conceal her nakedness. Apparently, the marshal and the madam shared a room at the Lotus Blossom.

"This ain't none of your affair, Hill!" declared the tenant of Room Seven. "So, step on back in that room with that whore and allow me to deal with this matter on my own terms."

"Being the acting law here in Hellbound, I'm sworn to make it my affair, Hardin," the elderly man retorted sternly.

Dead-Eye cocked an eyebrow. "Hardin? John Wesley Hardin? I saw a wanted poster for you back in Socorro."

"Is that right?" A dark challenge gleamed in the man's eyes. "You aim-ing to collect the bounty? If so, I'll correct my mistake of a few minutes ago and kill you for certain this time!"

"Nobody's going to collect any bounty money or shoot anyone," Boot Hill told him. He noticed the twin wounds in Dead-Eye's temples. "Well, not a second time, anyhow."

The dead man looked perturbed. "I'm not accustomed to being assaulted in such a way and the culprit not paying for it, either with jail time or a few bullet holes in return!"

"Here, here!" barked Boot Hill. "Now, why don't we all settle down, retire to our rooms, and get a decent night's sleep. Nobody ended up get-ting killed and it'd be to all our advantage if it remained that way." The marshal regarded the dark-haired man. "Are you intending to stay in Hellbound long, Hardin?"

"I'll be heading east for Colorado at daybreak," he replied, uncocking the big Russian revolver. "I'm game with burying the hatchet and making peace, but if they awaken me from a sound sleep again tonight, I may just ventilate the wall and, this time, hit who the lead is truly intended for!"

"I'll do my best to curtail my nasal expulsions," agreed Job, who looked like he was good and ready to leave the hallway and return to the warm folds of his bed.

John Wesley Hardin glared at the little black man and nodded curtly. "So be it!" Then he stepped back into his room and slammed the door.

Dead-Eye regarded the U.S. marshal with aggravation. "I do declare! I've never run across a lawman who wouldn't take action on a man being shot in the dead of night… particularly if the shooter was wanted by the authorities!"

"Sometimes, that's part of being a peace officer," Boot Hill told him defensively. "Keeping the peace. It'd do none of us a bit of good if we had a full-blown gunbattle right here in the hallway. Now, do as I suggested. Get back to your room and put this matter behind you." With that, he and Miss Flossie retired to their chambers and closed the door behind them.

When they were back in their room, Dead-Eye brooded as he returned to his straight-backed chair.

"Quit your pouting!" Job told him. The mojo man found a couple of bottle corks in his saddlebags and plugged the bullet holes in his partner's head, at least until they could be repaired properly. Then he prepared for bed for the second time that night. "Avoiding chaos makes for a restful night. If it makes you feel any better, I'm sorry you didn't get to murder someone. I know that goes against your nature these days."

"It's Boot Hill who's got me vexed," said Dead-Eye. "I could swear he backed down from Hardin out of fear. He's sure not the fella those dime novels painted him out to be!"

Job sat on the edge of the bed, his face serious. "Could be he has a good reason for declining trouble. Did you take a look at his hands?"

"No. Why should I?"

"They were all twisted up with arthritis," the negro told him. "His knuckles were swollen twice their size and at least three fingers on each hand were crooked and off center. I'd wager he would have a difficult time drawing a pistol and cocking it, let alone doing it fast and accurately."

Dead-Eye considered the revelation. "If he was in such poor condition, why did he agree to take on a position as constable in a vile and malicious town such as Hellbound?"

"Possibly because if he simply allows the riffraff and rabble to do as they please, he knows he won't be courting disaster or certain demise. In a decent, law-abiding town it would be the opposite. The townsfolk would hold him accountable... expect him to keep the peace and deal with troublemakers and scallywags accordingly. He's biding his final years safely in a place that holds no calamity or grievous circumstances for him... if he simply stays put and does nothing to buck the pony."

"I'm beginning to believe you're correct in your thinking," agreed Dead-Eye as Job climbed beneath the bedcovers and extinguished the lamp on the night table. "Must be a blight on a man's pride, living most of his life lifted up to God's stature and standing, when he's no more than a frightened old man stoved up with stiff joints, afraid that one wrong word or move might condemn him to death. If that happened, Boot Hill would not only be his namesake, but more than likely his final resting place."

Chapter Seventeen

The Poindexter Ranch
Seven miles west of Hellbound
November 1870

The following morning, Dead-Eye and Job left the hotel to find Boot Hill waiting for them on the walkway out front.

"I smell smoke," said the little mojo man. The faint odor of a fire hung about the town, although the source of it didn't seem to be within the boundaries of Hellbound, as far as he could tell.

The marshal nodded toward the end of the street. Beyond the town's buildings, off toward the western horizon, was a thick column of black smoke rising skyward. "Charlie Poindexter's ranch is out that way. Looks like there's been some trouble." Hill regarded the two and quickly voiced his intentions. "I was wondering if you'd mind riding out there with me to check on them. You have no obligation to do so, but being the only lawman in Hellbound—hell, possibly the only one in this part of the territory—I'm at a loss for decent men to deputize."

"You can keep your tin star," Dead-Eye told him. "I'll not have the responsibility of adhering to the law hinder me... particularly if I find need to draw my guns and do something contrary to it. But I'll go with you, if you need me."

"Do you believe this has something to do with Morgan Creed and the Hedgepaths leaving the saloon so early last night?" asked Job.

"That could very well be," replied Hill. "Poindexter has several corrals of mares and stallions on his place; sixty or more, I'd say. They'd be a mighty tempting haul for horse thieves like those four."

"You mind if I grab a bite of breakfast at the restaurant before we leave?" The black man's stomach rumbled hungrily.

Boot Hill handed him something wrapped in butcher's paper. "I had the cook slap some ham on a biscuit for you." He turned his eyes to Dead-Eye. "I'd wager you don't eat at all, do you?"

"If he did, the worms and shit beetles in his innards would likely wrestle each other for every bite he swallowed," Job told him.

They turned to see the blacksmith, Woody McClanahan, riding a gray quarter horse stout enough to tote his bulk. He wore a deputy's star on the breast of his shirt and was leading Balaam and Brimstone behind him.

"I took the liberty of having Woody saddle your animals," said the marshal. "He'll be coming with us."

"Then I reckon we don't have much choice in the matter." Dead-Eye swung atop the black Morgan, while Job slid his Henry rifle into its scabbard and mounted the albino mule.

An hour later, they reached the Poindexter ranch. The spread was located in an arid valley with a tall ridge of red rock behind it. There wasn't much left of the place. The four corrals were empty and the main house had been burnt to the ground. Only a jagged framework of blackened timbers remained, still laced with flame and sending a thick plume of smoke and ash into the cloudless Arizona sky.

Two bodies were lying in the yard out front of the burnt-out structure. Both had been set afire and charred to the bone. Bullet holes pocked their scorched skulls, and tatters of material from a calico dress lay around the smaller set of remains. Apparently, the marauders had taken liberties with the second victim before killing her.

Boot Hill's face grew pale at the sight of the two. "Charlie and his wife Millicent." Grimly, he looked toward the ruins of the house. Amid the smoke and flames, they could see a blackened crib smoldering in the rubble. "They had three young'uns. Twin girls, about four years of age, and a newborn baby boy."

As they sat on their horses and surveyed the devastation that had stricken the desert ranch in the dead of night, Woody broke away from the others and rode to examine the empty corrals. "They herded the horses toward that ridge yonder, and not very long ago," hollered the blacksmith. "Could be that we might catch up with them, if we ride hard."

"We'll return later and give Charlie and his family a proper burial," Hill said. "Right now, let's find those murderous swine and give them a taste of what they dished out to these poor folks!"

"You intending on doing it in a legal and morally-upright manner?" Dead-Eye asked.

Boot Hill unpinned his badge from his coat lapel and slipped it into his pocket, out of sight. "Hell no!"

Soon, the four of them were riding at a gallop in the direction of the ridge. They were scarcely a hundred yards away when rifle shots rang out from above. A bullet pierced the brim of the marshal's hat and punched a hole through the meat of his ear. It continued downward at a sharp angle, cutting a furrow across his shoulder blade and piercing the right flank of his horse. Hoping the others wouldn't notice, he held one of his pearl-gripped revolvers awkwardly in his right hand, fanning back the hammer with the heel of his left.

Dead-Eye lifted his Dragoon and snapped off a couple of shots. As the bullets hit the stone lip of the ridge, a Winchester repeater unleased a volley of gunfire. The zombie rocked back in his saddle as .44-40 slugs tunneled through his chest and belly. "There goes another damn shirt!" he cursed, then regained his balance and continued to fire.

Woody McClanahan roared in rage and spurred the big quarter forward at a sprint. He brandished a Navy Colt in each hand, allowing his horse to charge on its own accord.

"Woody, you fool!" shouted Hill. "Get your ass back here!"

"Charlie was a friend of mine!" the blacksmith yelled over his broad shoulder. "I'll be damned if they get away with what they've done!"

McClanahan was nearly to the base of the ridge, when something spun, end over end, from the top of the bluff, trailing sputtering flame and smoke in its wake. The blacksmith couldn't figure out what it was until it hit the ground, bounced, and landed beneath his horse's hooves.

The others watched, too far away to act, as the stick of dynamite detonated. It exploded in an ear-piercing roar, engulfing horse and rider in an eruption of black powder and fire. As the inferno subsided, debris lost momentum and began to fall to the earth. Some of it was dirt and stone, but most was human and equine in nature.

Cautiously, Dead-Eye, Job, and Boot Hill rode to where the explosion took place. They half expected lead to rain down upon their heads, but there was no further gunfire, only the lingering thunder of the powder blast echoing in their ears.

The area was scattered with dislodged rock, scorched vegetation, and smoldering fragments of the quarter horse lying about. Frantically, they looked about and found Woody McClanahan two hundred feet from where he'd last been. Or, rather, some of him.

Hill swung down from his horse and crouched next to the dying man. The blacksmith had been blown in half below the ribcage. His torn and rupture entrails fanned across the bloody earth around him. Both arms had been blown away, one just above the elbow and the other at the joint of his shoulder. "Good Lord, Woody!" the lawman said, laying a hand gently on the man's chest. "Look what they've gone and done to you!"

Blood gurgled past McClanahan's lips and dribbled down his chin. "I reckon I was too big a target to miss."

Dead-Eye swung down from Brimstone and looked quickly to the mojo man. "Job?"

The negro shook his head grimly. "There ain't nothing I can do for him. He's been torn all asunder."

Woody looked into the concerned eyes of J.B. Hill. "My end is near, Boot. I can feel it a-coming."

"I'm sorry, son. I don't how we'll be able to haul you back to Hellbound for burial, but we'll figure something out."

"Don't you dare!" groaned the big man. "Don't forget what we discussed this morning. I'll no longer be a part of that place, living or dead. Dig me a hole and bury what's left of me out here. I'd rather rest in peace in the wilderness, than toss and turn in my grave for eternity among murderers and thieves!"

Then, with a wet gasp and a shuddering sigh, Woody McClanahan gave up the ghost and was gone.

A quarter hour later, the three reached the summit of the ridge overlooking the Poindexter ranch. The spot was deserted. Only the milling trace of horse tracks in the dust and a multitude of spent cartridge casings were evidence that anyone had even been there.

The ridge was narrow, with scarcely two hundred feet distance from one side to the other. "I reckon Creed and the brothers must have made their escape down the other side."

Job sat atop Balaam and looked down into the vast stretch of desert that lay to the north. "Come take a look at this," he called to the lawman.

Boot Hill and Dead-Eye rode over and joined him. They peered into the valley below and was surprised at what they saw. In the scrubby wilderness below stood five dozen horses or so, not wild, but marked with the Poindexter brand of PDX in a circle.

"Well, I'll be damned!" said the elderly marshal. "From the looks of it, they took nary a one of them!"

"I believe it was all a ruse," Job told him. "They killed that family, set fire to the place, and emptied those corrals as bait. They wanted you to ride out here alone to investigate."

"They had an ambush in mind," said Dead-Eye with a nod. "But they didn't figure on us showing up alongside you."

Rage boiled in Hill's aged eyes. "All these innocent folks… Charlie and his family… Woody McClanahan… dead, because of me."

Dead-Eye and Job looked at one another. They thought of the bodies of all the victims Jules Holland, Evangeline, and the three demonic henchmen had left in their wake to taunt them and serve as a deadly warning. The circumstances were different, but they knew exactly how he felt.

The tall Southerner recalled Woody McClanahan's final words. "Boot, what did Woody mean by 'what we discussed this morning'? Was he intending to up and leave Hellbound?"

The lawman's face was solemn. "To tell the truth, several of us were. Some of the more civilized and trustworthy folks in town shared breakfast with me this morning. Woody, Minnie Graves, Hung Lo, and Miss Flossie. They've had enough of the killing and thievery that's been going on. Flossie most of all. The Hedgepaths have been taking her girls by force every night, beating the hell out of them and poking without paying, which is no more than rape in my book. We planned on packing up and moving on first thing tomorrow morning. Maybe to Nevada or as far as California. Looks like we'll be one man short on our journey, however."

"I reckon we ought to round up those horses and get them back to their pens," suggested Job. "Then we have graves to dig."

"They neglected to burn some of Poindexter's outbuildings," said Hill. "I figure there's a shovel and pick in one that we might make use of."

Dead-Eye noticed the marshal's hands for the first time since Job had mentioned them the night before. They were in much worse shape than he had pictured them to be. "I'll do the digging. In my present condition, I don't tucker out like normal folks. I reckon I could shovel to China and back without breaking a sweat, if need be."

Boot Hill nodded gratefully. "Much obliged."

Then, together, they rode down to attend to what needed to be done.

Chapter Eighteen

Main Street
Hellbound
November 1870

"Hold still!" scolded Miss Flossie. The redhead gently dabbed medicinal salve on the bullet hole in Boot Hill's ear and the ugly, three-inch furrow the bullet had cut across his upper back.

"It hurts like hell, dammit!" snapped the marshal with a grimace.

"You'd best let her attend to you," Job told him. "I concocted that salve myself from manglier root, goat weed, and lizard's tail. It'll heal those wounds up twice as fast as storebought."

"I can lend you a bullet to bite on, if you'd like," Dead-Eye suggested.

"The way these wounds are smarting, I'd likely bite one in half and blow my tongue clean off!"

"That might just be a blessing," the madam said. "Then I wouldn't have to listen to your bitching and complaining after we get hitched!"

"Well, I declare!" Job exclaimed. "When did this happen?"

"Last night," admitted Hill with a grin. "Gonna make her an honest woman as soon as we reach the next town." He eyed the gunfighter and the mojo man. "So, will you be riding out with us in the morning?"

Job looked over at Dead-Eye. "I reckon that depends on this fella here."

The dead man shook his head grimly. "I reckon I'll be sticking around to confront Creed and the Hedgepaths when they return. I can't allow them to get away with what they did to the Poindexters and McClanahan.

And, as far as Creed himself is concerned, I'll no longer tolerate what he did to me years ago." He regarded the marshal with a scowl. "I'd think you'd want to remain and see justice done, as well."

Boot Hill reached out and took Flossie's free hand. "I know it seems the cowardly thing to do, but I'm sick and tired of allowing this bullshit legend of mine rule my every thought and step. All the time afraid of what folks might think of me or want to do to me to test all those exaggerated lies and tall-tales. Truth is, I'm a crippled old man who just wants to give this badge a toss and settle down. With Flossie by my side, I can do that."

Dead-Eye nodded. "I suppose I can't rebuke you for that. I hope you both find the peace you're looking for."

When they'd said their goodbyes and Dead-Eye and Job had returned to their room, the tall Southerner seemed unusually quiet and troubled.

"What's on your mind?" Job wanted to know.

"You don't suppose John Legion is in cahoots with Creed and those Hedgepath boys, do you?

"I think if he was, Boot Hill's fate would have been sealed back there at the Poindexter ranch. No, whatever Legion has in mind, it'll be executed by him alone. Whether his bounty is the good marshal or not, I have no idea."

That night, Dead-Eye found himself back in Hell again.

He had been forced brutally to his knees, his wrists shackled to a block of limestone stained with the blood of a thousand men. His back was an open wound of shredded flesh, torn muscle, and raw, throbbing nerves. His own screams, sharp with agony and despair, still rang in his ears.

"Take a look, Wingade," whispered the voice of the Devil. "Look at what you've given me at the end of this whip."

Exhausted, Joshua lifted his head and stared at the tips of the leather straps. Clinging to the tenpenny nails and fragments of glass tied there was fresh blood and stringy bits of meat flayed from his back.

"Do you know your Bible, Wingade?" rasped Sergeant Creed in his ear. "It's what they called a cat o' nine tails. The Romans used it to scourge the body of Christ

before crucifixion. Its construction and purpose is to inflict unbearable pain and permanent damage. You sure as hell ain't Jesus. You're just a lowly worm of a traitorous reb placed in my custody, to do with as I please. To suffer and lament at my discretion. You will die a shallow and broken man in this place, Wingade. I'll do everything in my power to strip away the pride and brashness of your privileged upbringing, and reduce you to the squirming, shrieking maggot that you truly are!"

Joshua Wingade could utter nothing in reply. He simply lowered his head to the whipping block and wept, praying not for mercy, but for death.

Dead-Eye jolted awake.

For a moment, the ghosts of raw wounds across his back haunted him. Then, the numbness of death replaced the ugly memory and he found himself sitting in pitch darkness.

Beyond the door of Room Eight, he heard noises in the night. The scuffling of footsteps. A low moan. Soft laughter, inspired more from cruelty than humor.

Slowly, he left his chair and moved to the brass bed. He laid a hand on Job's shoulder. "Wake up," he said softly.

The mojo man opened his eyes. "What is it?"

"There's a commotion in the hallway. Someone's up to no good from the sound of it."

Silently, Job rose, dressed, and pulled on his mule-eared boots. He perched his derby hat atop his bald head and took the Henry repeater from where it leaned against a wall. As they crossed the room to the door, Dead-Eye drew his revolver and cocked the hammer. Since their unforeseen encounter with John Legion the night before, he had loaded the gun's cylinder with alternating cartridges bearing lead and silver.

They listened for a moment, but heard nothing. Quietly, they opened the door and stepped into the corridor. Instantly, they saw two things that disturbed them. The first were splatters of freshly-let blood on the hallway floor. The second was that the door opposite theirs—the one belonging to Boot Hill and his lady—stood partially open.

Dead-Eye moved forward and pushed the door open. "Boot?" he called out. "Miss Flossie?"

The darkness of the room was deathly silent. As their eyes grew accustomed to the gloom, they detected that someone was lying in the bed near the window. Job made his way to the nightstand and, lifting the chimney of a coal oil lamp, lit its wick.

The glow of the flame revealed a ghastly scene. Flossie's plump form lay sprawled across the bed, her nakedness partially concealed by tangled bedcovers. Her eyes were wide and full of terror. Someone had cut her throat open clear down to the neckbone.

John "Boot" Hill was nowhere to be found. A generous amount of blood stained his pillow and the rug beside the bed, trailing across the floor to the hallway.

"Creed and his lunatic bunch were here," said Dead-Eye. "They've made off with the marshal." He spotted the lawman's gun belt draped over the arm of a chair. "Grab those guns. We may have need of them."

Job nodded. He took the belt with the holstered revolvers. Rather than tote the rig across his shoulder, he buckled it around his waist.

Together, they left the room and rushed down the stairway to the hotel's lobby. Lo Hung, the proprietor of the Lotus Blossom, was absent from his post.

With their guns cocked and ready, the two stepped outside into the cool Arizona night. It didn't take them very long to discover what was going on.

A few yards past the livery stable, a bonfire had been stoked with lumber from the funeral parlor's side yard and ignited in the center of Hellbound's main street. The sturdy wench beam of the barn's hayloft had been used as a makeshift gallows. It was who was suspended there that filled their hearts with dread.

Boot Hill dangled from a noose, six feet off the ground. He was still dressed in his nightshirt, and his battered face was swollen and purple from strangulation. Dead-Eye considered shooting the rope above his head, but knew the act would be pointless. He could tell that the man was already dead.

"Pretty, ain't he?" said a voice from behind. "I was hoping to best him in a gunfight, but the old buzzard couldn't even find his pistols in the dark. We had our orders, anyway. Drag him out and string him up."

Slowly, Dead-Eye turned and faced the one who spoke. It was Cain, the eldest of the Hedgepath brothers. One of the others, Abel more than likely, flanked him on the left. The third sibling was nowhere to be seen.

"Allow me to face you in his stead," he said coldly. "I owe the gentleman that much, at least." The dead man slid his Dragoon pistol back into its holster and let his right hand hang loosely by his side.

Cain leered with a lopsided grin. His right hand was poised like a tanned spider above the butt of a holstered Remington. "I reckon I should warn you. When that crazy sawbones butchered our brainpans, he gave me reflexes like a damn diamondback!"

"Just shut the hell up and draw," rasped Dead-Eye.

The two men faced one another a couple of seconds more, then Cain Hedgepath dipped his hand and skinned the pistol with a snickering laugh. At the same instant, Dead-Eye already had the forty-four Colt in his grasp and was pulling the trigger. The bullet traveled the twenty paces between him and Cain, entering the muzzle of the Remington as it rose into line at the outlaw's hip. The cartridge exploded in the revolver's chamber as its hammer and Dead-Eye's slug struck the round at the same time. The gun exploded in a burst of burnt powder and twisted steel, taking off Cain's thumb and forefinger at the knuckles.

"You wouldn't have boasted so brashly if you'd known how many frigging rattlers I've defanged in my time," the zombie told him, then snapped off two more shots. The bullets hit Cain in the throat and just above the bridge of his nose. The misshapen man dropped backward, dead before he touched the earth of the street.

Dead-Eye was swinging his muzzle toward Abel, when the fellow fired first. The slug burrowed into his gun hand, ripping through putrid flesh and muscle, shearing his thumb clean off. It and the big Dragoon fell into the dust. The dead man lunged for the revolver with his left hand, but a second shot from Abel knocked the gun six feet away, completely out of his grasp.

"I know you're dead and that you can't be killed," said Abel, his eyes wild with rage. "But I can cut down that stubby brown bastard you hold so high in regard." And with that, he directed the muzzle of his pistol toward the center of Job's chest.

Before he could fire, however, a shadowy figure loomed out of the night. Lo Hung spun like a top, planting the sole of his foot forcefully into Abel Hedgepath's lower back. The man's spine shattered with a loud *crack*. The outlaw's face grew deathly pale with shock as his midsection folded in on itself like the blade of a pocketknife. He pitched over and sank to the street, his gun discharging into the dirt as he went. Before he could cock the hammer a second time, the Asian man flipped in the air like a carnival acrobat and brought his other foot downward with everything he could muster. It crushed the vertebrae in Abel's neck, twisting his head in the opposite direction of the rest of him.

"Dead-Eye," Job's voice said evenly. There was a tone of dire warning and resignation in its tone.

The Southerner turned around and faced the other way. There, standing in front of the bonfire, was Morgan Creed. He didn't brandish a firearm, but something much more threatening in nature. In one hand he held the stub of his cigar, while in the other he held a stick of dynamite.

"Looks like we were brought back together for a reason, Wingade," he said with a vindictive smile. "Maybe it was so I could finally finish what the War saved you from when they opened those prison doors at Camp Chase and released you from my possession. My objective was to strip away every last bit of spirit and humanity, and destroy you. Now I intend to complete my mission, right here and now."

"I ain't the best shot in the world," said Job, "but I reckon I can gut shoot that big belly of yours before you can touch off that fuse." Dead-Eye looked over and saw his partner holding one of Boot Hill's pearl-handled pistols.

"You thumb back that hammer, jigaboo, and I'll blow you clean off your feet!" They looked over and saw Seth, the final Hedgepath brother, standing in the shadows to the right. He held a double-barreled shotgun in his hands, aimed directly at Job's head.

"Looks like we're holding the ace after all," said Creed. He locked eyes with his adversary. "You may be faster than greased lightning with a pistol, Wingade… but I'd wager that you can't run as fast as you draw." His grin broadened and, with a laugh, he brought the glowing tip of the cigar toward the dry wick of the dynamite.

It was at that moment Dead-Eye looked past Creed and saw a dark form emerge from the heart of the bonfire.

The cigar was a fraction of an inch from igniting the stick of explosive, when the expression of ruthless triumph on Morgan Creed's face abruptly evaporated. In its place was a wide-eyed look of agony and sheer panic. Dead-Eye and Job watched as a red-hot point pierced the center of the man's chest, emerging with a burst of sulfurous smoke and boiling blood.

Creed screamed harshly as he was slowly lifted off his feet, revealing the one responsible for his unexpected fate.

John Legion—or, rather, a hellish incarnation of the otherworldly bounty hunter—stood directly behind him. The being's hair was no longer sleek and black, but a flowing, crackling mane of pure fire. His eyes held no pupils; they blazed brightly with an internal inferno born of Hell itself. The gleaming black coat had burnt and crumbled away, revealing his right arm, which had been transformed into something half serpent and half sword. The curved blade, as red and hot as a locomotive's furnace, held the former prison guard aloft, impaling him between his shoulder blades and emerging clear through the sternum of his ribcage.

"So, it was Creed you came to take," said Dead-Eye. A grim satisfaction etched his gaunt, mustachioed face.

"Yes!" said Legion. He held the man, kicking and screaming, for a moment, then flung him to the earth with contempt. Creed knelt there, his open mouth emitting a swarm of hot cinder and smoke, and his eyes melting in the pits of their sockets, as though he was being consumed by flame from the inside out. "Tell me, Dead-Eye, would you rather see this man die instantly from a single bullet… or suffer throughout eternity, mercilessly tormented by my kind, just as he tormented you and yours during the time of your imprisonment?"

The gunfighter couldn't help but concede to the notion. "I'd say that would be more fitting and irrevocable than anything I could subject him to."

A loud *clang* sounded from their right. Dead-Eye and Job glanced over to see the final Hedgepath brother crumbling to the street. Minnie Graves had sneaked up behind him and cleaved his skull in half, from crown to nose bone, with the edge of a burial spade.

"Many hated this man named Morgan Creed, but none as vehemently as an elderly grandmother in the mountains of Eastern Kentucky," Legion said. The fiery blade that had impaled the outlaw retracted, leaving only the bounty hunter's elaborately tattooed arm. "Her grandson was an innocent boy named Danny Johnson, who fought for his family's honor on the side of the Gray. He was captured following the battle of Mechanicsville and condemned to this devil's fiendish custody. The child, scarcely sixteen years of age, was brutalized physically and violated in the most deviant ways imaginable. After his release from that fetid hellhole, he returned home a shattered young man. Unable to live with the humiliation and shame he carried around inside him, he cast himself off a railroad trestle into the depths of the Red River Gorge and perished. The grandmother who loved him dearly was herself a witch and purveyor of mountain magic. She summoned me forth and forfeited her very soul in payment for retribution. And so, I have accomplished that task this night."

Dead-Eye nodded in approval. The death-dried flesh of his face creaked and crackled as he flashed a skeletal grin. "Her desire for vengeance shall serve as an equal portion for all who suffered and died at his hand. Just promise me one thing."

"And that is?"

The dead man walked over, retrieved the stick of dynamite Creed had dropped, and regarded it thoughtfully. "Allow him not a moment's peace or reprieve from the horrors you have in store for him."

John Legion seemed pleased with the zombie's request. "You have my word."

They watched as the bounty hunter grabbed Morgan Creed by the back of his neck and hauled him, shrieking and flailing, into the sweltering depths of the bonfire. From within the flames, a multitude of ghoulish arms, blistered and charred, embraced the sadistic prison guard, hauling him into the fiery pit of their realm.

Before he followed, Legion locked eyes with the man called Dead-Eye. "Heed my word. It is not settled between us. I will be back to collect the bounty the dark enchantress has commissioned upon your head."

"And I will be ready and waiting to dispute that claim," the gunman in black told him without a trace of fear or concern.

Then, a moment later, John Legion had stepped back into the flames and was swallowed whole.

"Given that this matter has been settled, what do you propose we do now?" asked Job. Lo Hung and Minnie Graves walked over and joined them, seeming dazed and at a loss at how to proceed.

Dead-Eye listened and heard a symphony of violence sweep throughout the night. Gunshots, the ripping and tearing of honed blades through flesh, and screams of agony and defeat echoed from the buildings and dark alleyways. It sounded as though the evil inhabitants of the Arizona town had been beguiled by some unseen force and were in the process of slaying one another, without restraint or mercy.

"Let's gather up the bodies of Boot Hill and Miss Flossie, locate those who wish to abandon this place, and then get to traveling," he said. "But, before we go, we'll make damn certain this accursed town perishes according to its namesake."

"So be it," Job agreed. "But before we do anything, run and fetch that thumb that was shot off. I'll stitch it back on, good as new." Pulling a silver-bladed knife from the cuff of his sleeve, the black man walked over and cut Seth Hedgepath's right hand off at the wrist.

"What'd you do that for?"

"The sort of luck you've been having these days," said Job, "it's always favorable to have a few spare parts on hand."

Daybreak found them on the trail heading westward.

Dead-Eye and Job rode point on Brimstone and Balaam. Following them was Minnie Graves driving an ebony hearse carriage drawn by two white horses, and a buckboard manned by Hung Lo. In the bed of the wagon sat the soiled doves of The Poisoned Waterhole Saloon, sorrowful at the loss of their benefactress, but relieved to be away from the purgatory they had been trapped in for the past several years.

A mile behind them, the town called Hellbound burned. The oddly-constructed buildings had been set on fire and, like dry tinder, had been swiftly consumed in flame. From a quick examination of the structures before their departure, they had discovered that every outlaw and murderer in town had killed one another, either due to an outbreak of homicidal fury of their own accord, or one mystically prompted by John Legion himself.

They paused and regarded the flames and billowing smoke from a distance. All found comfort in its fiery fate. Its demise put an end to a dark time in all their lives.

Later that day, they reached a crossroad. "I reckon we'll be heading northward for Wyoming," said Job. "We've heard that Jules Holland and his followers were seen heading that way. Where are you off to?"

"Virginia City," said Hung Lo. "I'm giving up opium as a trade. I'll see if my brother will teach me the art of cooking, if he'll even give me the time of day." He nodded over his shoulder at the girls in the bed of the wagon. "These ladies will be seeking more respectable employment as well. It's about time they work for themselves and not be treated as slaves, only worthy of an hour or two bouncing the bedsprings."

"Amen to that," agreed Job.

Dead-Eye regarded the two forms wrapped in white linen in the back of the hearse. "And what will become of Boot Hill and Miss Flossie?"

"We'll find them a peaceful, little spot in the desert," Minnie promised. "A shady place surrounded by juniper and flowering cactus, beside a waterhole. An oasis… or as close to one as we can find."

The gunfighter reached into his coat pocket, found something among the shotgun shells there, and tossed it to the lady mortician. It was the badge of a U.S. Marshal. "I found that on the floor of the hallway before we left. When you carve him a headstone, make sure that's nailed onto it. We knew the man as he truly was, but we'll keep that to ourselves. As far as everyone else is concerned, Boot Hill was, and always will be, a damn legend."

After all had said their farewells, they split ranks and went their separate ways. Soon, the clop of horse hooves and the squeak of wagon wheels faded, and Dead-Eye and Job were aware they were on their own once again.

They rode in silence for a long while. Then Job spoke.

"Looks to me like nothing stands in our way now. Not the deliverance of a small child, a promise of vengeance, or an old vendetta festering to be justified. It's only us and those we pursue."

Dead-Eye looked over at the little mojo man and nodded. "Then let's chase those scoundrels straight into the mouth of Hell." And, with that, he spurred Brimstone forward at a gallop.

Job let out a hoot and holler, and, with a crack of his reins, sent the white mule on its way. Soon, they were side by side, riding hell bent for leather in the shimmering desert heat.

Chapter Nineteen

The Valley of Fire
Northern Nevada
January 1871

"Good God Almighty!" Job peered through the eyepiece of his spy-glass and shook his head in disbelief. "It's five times the size that it was before!"

"Let me have a look-see." Dead-Eye took the telescope and lifted it to his good eye. "Yep. Looks like he's been sucking up every living thing in sight, that's for sure."

The two stood atop a curved ridge of smooth sandstone infused with layers of red, orange, and pink. The entire landscape, for as far as the eye could see, held the same assortment of fiery hues. That was why the Paiute and Shoshone called that stretch of desert the Valley of Fire.

In a rocky valley below, the behemoth known as Dolthemar slithered across the earth, leaving a trail of congealed blood behind it. When they had encountered it in New Mexico, it had been the size of a small cabin. Now its bulk had swollen to the size of a train depot. It was clear to see that it had captured and assimilated many creatures, both otherworldly and earthly, before it had found them.

"YOUR REPREIVE HAS COME TO AN END!" roared the fiend. "SURRENDER YOURSELVES AND BECOME ONE WITH ME!"

Dead-Eye flinched at the bellowing proclamation. "Well, he's sure as hell gotten louder, that's for sure. Must've tacked on at least another hundred mouths or so. And assholes, from the smell of it!" He looked over at Job. "So, have you figured out some way to defeat this gluttonous pest?"

"Well, we've got several options," the mojo man said. He took the little leather book from a vest pocket and began to flip through the pages. I could curse it with leprosy, but it'd take a while before it started rotting and losing its parts. Inflicting it with boils wouldn't work and conjuring a rash of gangrene would just make it stink even worse than it does now. I'm not sure if I can conjure a swarm of locust twice with the Staff of Moses. Might try another plague. Maybe gnats or frogs."

"It'd just swallow them whole," Dead-Eye told him. "Too bad we don't have another sacrifice to derail him like Father Núñez did before. You could give it a try. Walk down there and offer him an ear or a big toe."

Job frowned, engrossed in the variety of spells and curses in the yellowed pages of his book. "This is serious business. There's gotta be something in here that will do the trick."

"Well, I'll tell you what. You just stay put and keep sorting out your choices," said Dead-Eye. He turned and walked toward Brimstone. "I'll just ride on down there and take care of it myself."

The mojo man looked up from his reading and laughed. "Why, pardon me for dillydallying so! And just what sort of magic do you have hidden up your sleeve?"

The Southerner swung atop the black Morgan. "You'll see. Keep one thing in mind, though. When you see me ride past that thing, you'd best duck behind that boulder yonder. If you don't, you'll regret it."

Job watched as he urged his horse down a pathway to the canyon at the western end of the valley. "Just don't go getting yourself swallowed up. That's one damn thing I can't fix!"

Soon, Dead-Eye was lost from sight among a jumble of tall outcroppings of red rock and jagged hoodoos. Job looked down at the mass of assimilated body parts that made up the creature named Dolthemar. The thing was growing nearer with every slithering move forward. Job was disturbed to see long, black tentacles sprout from the brute and grab a couple of jackrabbits and a prairie dog, then add the squealing, protesting critters to its bodily collection.

"YOUR TARRYING IS TRYING MY PATIENCE!" the beast roared. Its thunderous voice reverberated off the rock walls and pinnacles of stone. "RELINQUISH YOUR FREEDOM AND FIND NEW PURPOSE AS AN ADDITION TO MY GLORIOUS MASS!"

Job flipped through the pages of his leatherbound book, searching for a solution. A calling forth of buzzards? he wondered. Hell, they could eat themselves full and still not make a dent!

It was at that moment he looked up and, several hundred yards behind the monster, saw Dead-Eye and Brimstone round a cluster of boulders at a full gallop. He was surprised to see no gun whatsoever in the zombie's hand, but rather something much more unexpected. The end of the object spat and sizzled with fire and smoke as he neared Dolthemar and flung it forcefully into the churning mass of raw viscera. Then he spurred the horse past the thing and, dodging a couple of the dark tentacles, headed straight for the ridge Job stood upon.

"Oh, shit!" The negro remembered the boulder and leapt behind it just in the nick of time.

An earth-shaking roar filled the desert air, along with a gory explosion of every bodily protrusion, organ, and appendage imaginable. When the thunderous report faded and the heavenly hail of sanguinary carnage gradually subsided, Job peeked out from behind the rock that sheltered him. All that was left of the being known as Dolthemar was a massive, bloody stain on the rocky earth of the valley floor.

A moment later, Dead-Eye joined him on the ridge. His coat and hat dripped with ichor and stray body parts. "I reckon that dynamite Creed was gonna heave at us came in handy after all."

Job shook his head in amazement. "Well, hell. That was... simple."

"It's often better to not complicate matters so."

"You mean, like shooting someone or blowing something to smithereens?"

Dead-Eye grinned. "Something like that."

Job pointed to the brim of the dead man's hat. "Uh, looks like you've got an ear lying there."

The gunfighter reached up and picked it off, intending to fling it away.

"Hold on." Job extended his hand, took the ear from Dead-Eye's hand, and examined it. It was dark brown in skin tone and a woman's in size, with a pearl earring in the lobe. "It may not be your color or gender, but it'll work if you should have need of it. At least it'd keep your hat from slipping over your eyes."

"Evangeline."

She smiled and opened her eyes. "Papa. You came to visit."

"You ain't the only one in the family who could dream-walk."

The young woman sat up. The interior of the wagon was as dark as death, but she could still see her father a few feet away, perched atop a steamer trunk. "I thought you didn't approve of such talents. You always were so stiff-necked and uncompromising. That's why Mama despised you at the end."

"If you call refusing to give in to darkness and wickedness uncompromising, then you're right. But I do allow myself to use witchery and black magic upon occasion, if it suits my needs."

Evangeline laughed. "You mean like raising that gutless weakling from the dead and bewitching his confounded horse?"

Job nodded. "Among other things, yes."

She smiled slyly. "Tell me, dear father, where are you now? Are you still roaming through the Mexican desert? Or are you closing the miles between our camp and yours?"

"I believe you know good and well where we are. If not, you wouldn't be sending your eldritch agents to halt our progress. By the way, that piece of rotting offal called Dolthemar has been destroyed."

Evangeline seemed startled. "You've slain the Collector? But how?"

Job's gold and silver teeth gleamed in the darkness. "We blew its ass to kingdom come... or wherever a pile of shit like that goes when it kicks the bucket. It was Dead-Eye who did it. Stepped in and annihilated the bastard when magic came up short."

The dark woman smiled. "Ah, the legendary Dead-Eye. Your avenging angel from beyond the grave." Cruelty gleamed in Evangeline's eyes. "Riding to save his precious son, even after all these years. If he only knew Daniel as he is now and what he has become at the tutelage of his surrogate father. You may deliver the heart-breaking news to him, if you'd like."

The mojo man's face grew troubled. "If that be the case, he'll discover it for himself when the time comes."

"If it is up to me, that time will never take place. For both of you will fall to death and degradation in the searing pits of Hell before you come within a hundred miles of me and my confederates."

"And, so, you shall continue to send your army of inhuman bounty hunters and reprobates through the Hole?" Job countered. "So far, they've not had much success at deterring our mission. Even if I end up perishing, Dead-Eye will refuse to stop. He will continue with his quest for his son and the unrelenting desire for vengeance that he craves."

Evangeline stroked the cursed tome that lay on the cot next to her. "Then perhaps I should delve deeper into these pages... call forth behemoths and leviathans from dark realms that no mortal could imagine... or tolerate to even comprehend. Perhaps I should leave more warnings in your wake, at the expense of the innocent."

Job shook his head sadly. "I once loved you, Evangeline. Of all my young'uns, you were the most precious in my eyes. But what you've become, what you've done with that monstrosity of a book you possess... well, I cannot abide that, nor allow it to continue."

The woman yawned. "You do prattle on and on, don't you? You've bored me with your threats and ultimatums, Papa. You and your precious judgment have overstayed your welcome."

A great sorrow shown in her father's eyes. "Then I've wasted my time in coming here. Farewell for now, daughter. The dreadful day when we truly meet face to face shall come... perhaps sooner than you think. And, on that day, I will mourn for your loss."

"The loss shall be your own, with no grief or regret on my part."

Then she watched as he slowly faded into the darkness.

Evangeline awoke with a start and lay there, recalling the encounter from moments before. Of the harsh words and bitterness that had passed between them.

The ancient book shuddered beneath her touch. Its binding of human flesh and yellowed parchment squirmed and rippled restlessly.

"Hush, my love," she whispered, with a gentle stroke of her hand. "Twas only a bad dream."

Necronomicon grew quiet at the soothing sound of her voice. It returned to its slumber and found solace in the dark words and obscene etchings within its ancient pages.

As long as it was in the possession of its dark mistress, it would serve her faithfully and willingly open forbidden doorways. Portals that gave access to vile worlds, malevolent deities, and chaos unfathomed, at the very coaxing of her voice.

TO BE CONTINUED...

About the Author

Ronald Kelly was born November 20, 1959, in Nashville, Tennessee where he was raised a Southern Baptist. He attended Pegram Elementary School and Cheatham County Central High School (both in Ashland City, Tennessee) before starting his writing career.

Ronald Kelly began his writing career in 1986 and quickly sold his first short story, "Breakfast Serial," to *Terror Time Again* magazine. His first novel, *Hindsight* was released by Zebra Books in 1990. His audiobook collection, *Dark Dixie: Tales of Southern Horror*, was on the nominating ballot of the 1992 Grammy Awards for Best Spoken Word or Non-Musical Album. Zebra published seven of Ronald Kelly's novels from 1990 to 1996. Ronald's short fiction work has been published by *Cemetery Dance, Borderlands 3, Deathrealm, Dark at Heart, Hot Blood: Seeds of Fear*, and many more. After selling hundreds of thousands of books, the bottom dropped out of the horror market in 1996. So, when Zebra dropped their horror line in October 1996, Ronald Kelly stopped writing for almost ten years and worked various jobs including welder, factory worker, production manager, drugstore manager, and custodian.

In 2006, Ronald Kelly started writing again. Since then, he has written and published several new novels (*Hell Hollow, Restless Shadows*, and *The Buzzard Zone*), numerous short story collections, and has become an elder statesman of Southern-Fried Horror in his chosen genre. In 2021, his collection of extreme horror tales, *The Essential Sick Stuff*, won the Splatterpunk Award for Best Collection. He is currently working on The Saga of Dead-Eye, a five-volume horror western series. Book One, Vampires, Zombies, & Mojo Men was recently published by Thunderstorm Books.

Ronald Kelly currently lives in a backwoods hollow in Brush Creek, Tennessee, with his wife and young'uns.

Novels

Blood Kin
Father's Little Helper (re-released as Twelve Gauge)
Fear
Hell Hollow
Hindsight
Moon of the Werewolf (re-released as Undertaker's Moon)
Pitfall
Restless Shadows
Something Out There (re-released as The Dark'Un)
The Buzzard Zone
The China Doll
The Possession (re-released as Burnt Magnolia)
The Saga of Dead-Eye, Book 1: Vampires, Zombies, & Mojo Men
The Saga of Dead-Eye, Book 2, Werewolves, Swamp Critters & Hellacious Haints.
Timber Gray

Novellas

Flesh Welder

Collections

After the Burn
Cumberland Furnace and Other Fear Forged Fables
Dark Dixie
Dark Dixie II
Haunt of Southern-Fried Fear
Irish Gothic: Tales of Celtic Horror
Long Chills
Midnight Tide & Other Seaside Stories
Mister Glow-Bones & Other Halloween Tales
More Sick Stuff
Season's Creepings: Tales of Holiday Horror
The Essential Sick Stuff
The Halloween Store and Other Tales of All Hallows' Eve
The Sick Stuff
The Web of La Sanguinaire and Other Arachnid Horrors
Twilight Hankerings
Unhinged

Curious about other Crossroad Press books?
Stop by our site:
https://www.crossroadpress.com
We offer quality writing
in digital, audio, and print formats.

www.ingramcontent.com/pod-product-compliance
Lightning Source LLC
Chambersburg PA
CBHW022029170626
46808CB00003B/1119